# The Mystery
# of the Coniunctio

Marie-Louise von Franz, Honorary Patron

**Studies in Jungian Psychology
by Jungian Analysts**

Daryl Sharp, General Editor

# The Mystery of
# THE CONIUNCTIO

## Alchemical Image
## of Individuation

Lectures by
**EDWARD F. EDINGER**
**Transcribed and Edited by Joan Dexter Blackmer**

The material in this book was first presented in lectures at
the C.G. Jung Institute of San Francisco, October 19-20, 1984.

**Canadian Cataloguing in Publication Data**

Edinger, Edward F. (Edward Ferdinand),
    The mystery of the coniunctio: alchemical image of individuation

(Studies in Jungian psychology by Jungian analysts; 65)

Includes bibliographical references and index.

ISBN 9780919123670

1. Jung, C.G. (Carl Gustav), 1875-1961.
2. Individuation (Psychology).
I. Blackmer, Joan Dexter.
II. Title. III. Series.

BF175.5.153E4 1994     150.19'54     C94-931481-1

INNER CITY BOOKS
21 Milroy Crescent, Toronto, Canada M1C 4B6
416-927-0355

Honorary Patron: Marie-Louise von Franz.
Publisher and General Editor: Daryl Sharp.
Senior Editor: Victoria Cowan.

INNER CITY BOOKS was founded in 1980 to promote the
understanding and practical application of the work of C.G. Jung.

*Cover:* "The Mandala Fountain," colorized woodcut from the
Frankfurt first edition of *Rosarium philosophorum* (1550).

Index by Daryl Sharp

Printed and bound in Canada by Rapido Livres Books
Reprinted 2025

# CONTENTS

*See final page for descriptions of other Inner City Books*

C.G. Jung in his study at the age of 85
(Photo by Karsh of Ottawa)

# 1

# Introduction to Jung's
## *Mysterium Coniunctionis*

I'm going to talk tonight about Jung's final work, *Mysterium Coniunctionis,* published as volume 14 of his *Collected Works.*

This superlative work is exceedingly difficult for us ordinary mortals. I think that's because it was written for the ages and not for current popularity. It was written out of a magnitude of psychic experience and breadth of view that none of us can match. However, I do feel that we cannot be true to Jung's legacy unless we make an earnest effort to understand *Mysterium.* I have made that effort and continue to do so, and I hope that what I have to say tonight will open it up for you sufficiently to encourage you to make a similar effort.

The subtitle of *Mysterium Coniunctionis* is "An Inquiry into the Separation and Synthesis of Psychic Opposites in Alchemy." One might ask, why alchemy? What is its relevance for the modern mind? And the answer is that alchemy gives us a unique glimpse into the depths of the unconscious psyche, a glimpse no other body of symbolism provides in quite the same way. Here's what Jung says about it in "The Philosophical Tree":

> [We] must turn back to those periods in human history when symbol forma-
> tion still went on unimpeded, that is, when there was still no epistemological
> criticism of the formation of the images, and when, in consequence, facts that
> in themselves were unknown could be expressed in definite visual form. The
> period of this kind closest to us is that of medieval natural philosophy, which
> . . . . attained its most significant development in alchemy and Hermetic
> philosophy.[1]

The alchemists were fired with the beginnings of the modern spirit of inquiry, but yet, as investigators of the nature of matter they were still half asleep. So, in their zeal to investigate those newly opened vistas, they projected their fantasies and dream images into matter. In effect, they

---

[1] *Alchemical Studies,* CW 13, par. 353. [CW refers throughout to *The Collected Works of C.G. Jung]*

Alchemists at work on various stages of the process
(Mutus liber, 1702)

dreamed a vast collective dream using chemical operations and materials as imagery and subject matter for that dream. Alchemy is that great collective dream, and what makes it so important for us is that it's the dream of our ancestors. The alchemists were rooted in the Western psyche which we've inherited, so their imagery, their fantasy, their dream, is our fantasy and our dream.

That's what Jung demonstrates so magnificently in his major works on alchemy. He shows that if we pay serious attention to alchemical images, we will find the same material that comes up in our dreams. That's why alchemy is worth considering. Before I venture into the subject matter, I want to tell you a story, one that Jung told. Here's what he said:

> I always remember a letter I received one morning, a poor scrap of paper, really, from a woman who wanted to see me just once in her life. The letter made a very strong impression on me, I am not quite sure why. I invited her to come and she came. She was very poor—poor intellectually too. I don't believe she had ever finished primary school. She kept house for her brother; they ran a little newsstand. I asked her kindly if she really understood my books which she said she had read. And she replied in this extraordinary way, "Your books are not books, Herr Professor, they are bread."[2]

To the pious Jew, the Torah is bread. To the believing Christian, the Gospels are bread. To the devout Muslim, the Koran is bread. Why is that? It's because all these scriptures are treasuries of the archetypes, each in its own religious and cultural context. *Mysterium Coniunctionis* belongs in this same company. It too is a treasury of the archetypes and it too is bread. Let me give you a few examples of how the archetypal psyche describes itself as bread.

In Deuteronomy we read: "[He] fed thee with manna . . . that he might make thee know that man doth not live by bread only, but by every word that proceedeth out of the mouth of the Lord."[3]

In Proverbs, Divine Wisdom says : "Come, eat of my bread."[4]

In Ecclesiasticus, it is said of Wisdom: "She will give him the bread of understanding to eat."[5]

Christ says of himself: "I am the living bread which came down from

---

[2] *C.G. Jung Speaking: Interviews and Encounters,* p. 416.

[3] Deut. 8: 3, Authorized Version.

[4] Prov. 9: 5, Authorized Version.

[5] Ecclesiasticus 15: 3, Jerusalem Bible.

heaven: if any man eat of this bread, he shall live forever."[6]

The Koran speaks of a table spread with food sent by Allah from heaven for the believers.[7]

The Philosophers' Stone of the alchemists is called a *cibus immortalis,* a food of immortality.[8]

*Mysterium Coniunctionis* belongs in this same category. It's bread for the psyche. I think that will be recognized by anyone who has a living connection with the unconscious and who consults this book for relevant imagery. The images here feed one's connection to the psyche and one's understanding of it. Another way of putting it would be to say that *Mysterium Coniunctionis* is a bible of the psyche. One doesn't read it from cover to cover. One consults it for understanding and amplification of a particular image. You read it word by word, verse by verse, and reflect on each sentence and on each image.

There's another way of describing this book. It's an anatomy book of the psyche, and I consider this a particularly enlightening parallel that I want to pursue a little further. To illustrate it, let me begin by reading you the first paragraph of *Mysterium.*

> The factors which come together in the coniunctio are conceived as opposites, either confronting one another in enmity or attracting one another in love. To begin with they form a dualism; for instance—the opposites are moist/dry, cold/warm, upper/lower, spirit-soul/ body, heaven/earth, fire/water, bright/dark, active/passive, volatile/solid, precious/cheap, good/evil, open/occult, East/West, living/dead, masculine/feminine, Sol/Luna. Often the polarity is arranged as a quaternity, with the two opposites crossing one another, as for instance the four elements or the four qualities (moist, dry, cold, warm), or the four directions and seasons, thus producing the cross as an emblem of the four elements and symbol of the sublunary physical world.[9]

Now, compare that with this passage from an anatomy text book:

> The sutures of the cranium seen on the vertex are the following: the *metopic suture* . . . merely a slight median fissure in the frontal bone just above the glabella. . . . The *sagittal suture* is situated between the two parietal bones. The single or paired *parietal foramen* lies close to the sagittal suture, a short distance anterior to the spot (lambda) where it joins the lambdoid suture. The *coronal suture* lies between the frontal bone anteriorly and the two parietal

---

[6] John 6: 51, Authorized Version.

[7] Koran, Sura V, 112.

[8] See, for instance, *Mysterium,* par. 525.

[9] Condensed, with Latin terms omitted.

bones posteriorly. The *lambdoid suture* is formed by the meeting of the parietal bones in front, and the occipital bone behind.[10]

My point is, I don't think you'll be able to follow this description unless you already know the anatomy of the cranium or have at hand an actual skull which you can examine in order to verify each statement by personal observation.

You see, the study of physical anatomy must be accompanied by the empirical experience of dissection, where you can witness the actual anatomical facts for yourself. And these same considerations apply to an understanding of *Mysterium Coniunctionis.* You really do need to have some experience of the psyche in order to know what Jung is talking about. When you read about the opposites, the four elements, the red man, the white woman, etc., they will mean no more than the coronal and sagittal sutures do to a person ignorant of anatomy.

So, for a full understanding of Jung, one must go to the dissecting room of the psyche. That of course is a personal analysis. But even if you haven't had a personal analysis, perhaps you can get some idea of the rich content of *Mysterium* from what I'm going to tell you about it.

Going back to that first paragraph, let's take just the first sentence. It reads as follows:

> The factors which come together in the coniunctio are conceived as opposites, either confronting one another in enmity or attracting one another in love.

This sentence tells us what the entire book is about. It's about the opposites; it's about enmity, and it's about love or desire. These are the matters I shall talk about tonight. Jung speaks to these matters chiefly in terms of the symbolic images they evoke as they emerge from the unconscious, but I shall speak of them chiefly from the standpoint of personal, conscious experience.

The opposites constitute the most basic anatomy of the psyche. The flow of libido, or psychic energy, is generated by the polarization of opposites in the same way as electricity flows between the positive and negative poles of an electrical circuit. So, whenever we are attracted toward a desired object, or react against a hated object, we're caught up in the drama of the opposites. The opposites are truly the dynamo of the psyche. They are the motor, they're what keeps the psyche alive.

---

[10] *Morris' Human Anatomy,* p. 104.

Now just having experiences of being attracted to things and repulsed by things does not constitute consciousness. Consciousness requires a simultaneous experience of opposites and the acceptance of that experience. And the greater the degree of this acceptance, the greater the consciousness.

It's interesting to go back in cultural history because we can locate almost exactly when the fact of the opposites came into recorded view. The opposites were discovered by the pre-Socratic philosophers, the Pythagoreans. I don't know that they discovered them exactly, but they did establish them as important entities, setting up a table of ten pairs of opposites they considered to be the basic ones.

Here's the list of ten Pythagorean opposites, a kind of signpost right at the beginning of the development of Western consciousness. The opposites that stood out most prominently for those early philosophers were these: limited/unlimited, odd/even, one/many, right/left, male/female, resting/moving, straight/curved, light/dark, good/bad, square/oblong.

I think the importance of the discovery of the opposites can hardly be overestimated. And, just as with numbers, there was an aura of numinosity about them when they were first discovered. They arose out of the unconscious and trailed clouds of the numinous from that other world. That was true of the early discovery of numbers, and it is also true of the discovery of opposites.

The world has to be rent asunder and the opposites must be separated, in order to create space in which the human conscious ego can exist. This is beautifully expressed in an ancient Egyptian myth which speaks of Nut, the sky goddess and Geb, the earth god, who were initially in a state of union, of perpetual cohabitation. Then Shu got between them and pushed them apart. That separated the heaven from the earth and created a sort of bubble of space in which the world could exist.[11]

This image is very much like what happens with the emergence of every young ego: it must push apart that which is pushing against it and

---

[11] See Edinger, *Anatomy of the Psyche,* pp. 185ff.

The separation of heaven and earth: Nut lifted above Geb by Shu[12]

make room for itself to exist. It must define itself as something different from its environment.

The young ego is obliged to establish itself as something definite and therefore it must say, "I *am* this and I am *not* that." No-saying is a crucial feature of initial ego development. But the result of this early operation is that a shadow is created. All that I announce I am *not* then goes into the shadow. And sooner or later, if psychic development is to occur, that split-off shadow must be encountered again as an inner reality; then one is confronted with the problem of the opposites that had earlier been split apart.

I would say that the most crucial and terrifying pair of opposites is good and evil. The very survival of the ego depends on how it relates to this matter. In order to survive, it is absolutely essential that the ego experience itself as more good than bad. There has to be a heavier weight on the side

---

[12] Drawing after an illustration in A. Jeremias, *Das Alte Testament im Lichte des Alten Orients* (Leipzig, 1904). Turin, Egyptian Museum. Reprinted in Erich Neumann, *The Origins and History of Consciousness.*

of good, in the balance, than on the side of evil. And this of course explains the creation of the shadow, for the young ego can tolerate very little experience of its own badness without succumbing to total demoralization. It also accounts for another universal phenomenon—the process of locating evil. Evil has to be located, it has to be fixed and established as residing in some particular spot. Whenever something bad happens, blame or responsibility must be established if at all possible. It is exceedingly dangerous to have free-floating evil. Someone must personally carry the burden of evil.[13]

As the ego matures, the situation gradually changes, and the individual becomes able to take on the task of being the carrier of evil. Then it is not so important to locate the evil elsewhere. When one is able to acknowledge one's evil, one becomes a carrier of the opposites, and in so doing contributes to the creation of the coniunctio.

In the early phase of the recognition of the opposites we have what might be called the pendulum stage. At this stage the individual is cast back and forth between different moods. On the one hand, there will be the mood of guilty inferiority, and when the pendulum swings there's an optimistic up-turn. And it can go back and forth between those two so that light and darkness are encountered one after another.

Jung makes a remarkable statement about this phenomenon in paragraph 206 of *Mysterium.* Listen to this:

> The one-after-another is a bearable prelude to the deeper knowledge of the side-by-side, for this is an incomparably more difficult problem. Again, the view that good and evil are spiritual forces outside us, and that man is caught in the conflict between them, is more bearable by far than the insight that the opposites are the ineradicable and indispensable preconditions of all psychic life, so much so that life itself is guilt.

This will perhaps give you some idea of what a grave matter it is to consider seriously the problem of the opposites. I don't believe it's over-stating it to say that an understanding of the opposites is the key to the psyche—but it's a dangerous key, because one is dealing with the elemental machinery of the psyche. If the machine is taken apart, one might not get it back together again. Nonetheless, the urge to individuation may require the individual to embark on this dangerous enterprise, which if successful also

---

[13] See Sylvia Brinton Perera, *The Scapegoat Complex: Toward a Mythology of Shadow and Guilt.*

offers the possibility of an increase in consciousness.

Once you start thinking about it, and once you become familiar with the phenomenon of the opposites, you'll see it everywhere. It's *the* basic drama that goes on in the collective psyche. Every war, every contest between groups, every dispute between political factions, every game, is an expression of coniunctio energies. Whenever we fall into an identification with one of a pair of warring opposites, we then lose the possibility, for the time being anyway, of being a carrier of the opposites. And instead we become one of God's millstones that grinds out fate. At such times one still locates the enemy on the outside and in so doing is simply a particle. As Emerson said:

> Is it not the chief disgrace in the world, not to be a unit; not to be reckoned one character; not to yield that peculiar fruit which each man was created to bear, but to be reckoned in the gross, in the hundred, or in the thousand, of the party, the section, to which we belong, and our opinion predicted geographically, as the north or the south?[14]

And Jung puts the same idea in different words:

> If the subjective consciousness prefers the ideas and opinions of collective consciousness and identifies with them, then the contents of the collective unconscious are repressed. . . . And the more highly charged the collective consciousness, the more the ego forfeits its practical importance. It is, as it were, absorbed by the opinions and tendencies of collective consciousness, and the result of that is the mass man, the every-ready victim of some wretched "ism." The ego keeps its integrity only if it does not identify with one of the opposites, and if it understands how to hold the balance between them. This is possible only if it remains conscious of both at once.[15]

I want to say a word or two about the psychology of sports and games, because I think it's quite relevant to our subject. Many years ago I found myself watching a lot of football on television and I wondered, "Why am I doing this?" I was caught in a kind of fascination, the fascination of collective consciousness, you see; I was a "mass man" as Jung spoke of it in the passage I just read. And as I reflected on it, it became perfectly evident to me that what goes on in the sports so many people watch on weekends is a kind of degraded sacred ritual.

Don't laugh; that's really true! Games were originally sacred, dedicated to the gods, and anything is sacred that acts out an archetypal drama.

---

[14] "The American Scholar," in *Selected Writings of Ralph Waldo Emerson,* p. 63.

[15] *The Structure and Dynamics of the Psyche,* CW 8, par. 425.

Sporting contests do act out the drama of the coniunctio. Each contestant strives to achieve victory and to avoid defeat, and yet one must win and one must lose. But within the vessel of the game, the opposites unite; and in the course of many contests, the players learn to assimilate both victory and defeat, and thus promote the inner coniunctio.

It is definitely not good psychologically always to be a winner, because then one is deprived of the full experience of the opposites. It keeps one superficial. Defeat is the gateway to the unconscious. All profound people have known defeat; it's a necessary part of the experience of the opposites.

Michelangelo paid a wonderful tribute to Dante, his countryman, in one of his sonnets. Speaking of Dante he said:

> He did not fear to plumb the places where
> Failure alone survives.[16]

You see, failure and guilt are necessary experiences because each is a part of wholeness. In order to experience the union of the opposites, you have to experience failure and guilt. I remember what a revelation it was to me the first time I came across this remark of Jung's:

> [In a person's life] there is something very like a *felix culpa* [a happy fault]. .
> . . One can miss not only one's happiness but also one's final guilt, without
> which a man will never reach his wholeness.[17]

In other places, too, Jung makes it very clear that he attaches value to guilt. We often try desperately to avoid consciousness of our guilt, and in doing so we're forced into shadow projection. Both shadow projection and factional identification are evidence of an immature ego (which of course is not helped by hostile criticism).

An image I find very helpful is to liken the ego to a fishing boat. Such a boat can take on only a certain amount of fish, no more than it can hold. The load must be commensurate with its size. What if you're fishing in a small row boat and catch a whale? If you pull it in, you'll go under. This is an apt image because the problem of the opposites is indeed a whale: grappling with the opposites leads directly to an encounter with the Self.

There's a beautiful account of this image in Melville's *Moby Dick.* The whole book is an expression of it, but at one point in the book Melville discusses the fact that the whale has eyes on opposite sides of its head and

---

[16] "Sonnet II," in *The Sonnets of Michelangelo,* p. 32.

[17] *Psychology and Alchemy,* CW 12, par. 36.

thus gets two completely different images of the nature of reality simulta-neously, two opposite images. Melville comments on what a grand and mysterious entity it must be that is able to unite the opposites, illustrating specifically how the whale, Moby Dick, is indeed a symbol of the Self.[18]

Now I grant you, only a few people are meant to go whale hunting. But, if you are one of those so destined, it is more dangerous to evade your task than it is to face it—because the whale will get you from behind.[19]

All right, how does one go about whale hunting? Where are the opposites to be found?

Well, you find them by scrutinizing whatever you love and hate. That's easy to say but I assure you it is exceedingly difficult to do. The reason it's so difficult is that whenever feelings of love or hate come upon us, they are not accompanied by inclinations to scrutiny. Remember the first sentence of *Mysterium Coniunctionis:*

> The factors which come together in the coniunctio are conceived as opposites, either confronting one another in enmity or attracting one another in love.

Whenever we take too concretely an urge to love or hate, then the con-iunctio is exteriorized and thereby destroyed. If we are gripped by a strong attraction to a person or a thing, we must reflect on it. As Jung says:

> Unless we prefer to be made fools of by our illusions, we shall, by carefully analysing every fascination, extract from it a portion of our own personality, like a quintessence, and slowly come to recognize that we meet ourselves time and again in a thousand disguises on the path of life.[20]

The same applies to our passionate antipathies. They also must be sub-jected to thorough analytic scrutiny. Whom do I hate? What groups or fac-tions do I fight against? Whoever and whatever they are, they are a part of me; I'm bound to that which I hate as surely as I am to that which I love. The important thing, psychologically, is where one's libido is lodged, not whether one is for or against a particular thing. If we follow such reflections diligently, very gradually we will collect our scattered psyche from the outer

---

[18] See Edinger, *Melville's Moby Dick: A Jungian Commentary (An American Nekyia),* pp. 78f.

[19] Recall Jung's advice using a different metaphor: "Anyone who is destined to descend into a deep pit had better set about it with all the necessary precautions rather than risk falling into the hole backwards." (*Aion,* CW 9ii, par. 125)

[20] "The Psychology of the Transference," *The Practice of Psychotherapy,* CW 16, par. 534.

world, as Isis gathered the dismembered body of Osiris, and in doing that we will be working on the coniunctio.

But turning now to that word, coniunctio. What does it mean? What is the coniunctio? That's the title of the book—*Mysterium Coniunctionis*—the Mystery of the Coniunctio or the Mysterious Coniunctio, or the Con-iunctio that is a Mystery.

According to alchemical symbolism, the coniunctio is the goal of the process; it's the entity, the stuff, the substance that is created by the alchemical procedure when finally it succeeds in uniting the opposites. It is a mysterious, transcendent thing that can be expressed by many symbolic images. Let me list some of the chief ones:

The Philosophers' Stone, a miraculous, incorruptible body which multiplies itself and turns base matter into noble matter, or into gold, or into more of itself.

The *aqua permanens,* which can be translated either as "permanent water" or "penetrating water"; it's the water that can penetrate everything. In alchemical writings it's also called the tincture, because it colors everything it penetrates—it affects everything with its own color.

A third term is the *filius philosophorum,* the son of the philosophers, a figure thought of as a savior of the world.

Another term is the *pharmakon athanasias,* the medicine of immortality. And sometimes it's called the *cibus immortalis,* food of immortality.

There are many more, but these are some major images. The symbolism is very complex and obscure, but tonight is not the time to go into the difficult symbolic details.[21] For our purposes now, I'm going to rashly tell you exactly how I see the coniunctio.

The coniunctio, and the process that creates it, I consider to represent the creation of consciousness, which is an enduring psychic substance created by the union of opposites. I go into this idea in considerable detail in *The Creation of Consciousness,* if you're interested. But the key word is "consciousness."

Now, as I use that word, I have the urge to characterize this consciousness. For instance, I'd like to call it higher consciousness, or maybe larger consciousness, but I may not do that because it would not be strictly true to the facts of the opposites. Because if it is a higher consciousness, it is also

---

[21] For fuller discussion see Edinger, *The Mysterium Lectures: A Journey Through C.G. Jung's* Mysterium Coniunctionis.

a lower consciousness; and if it's a larger consciousness, it's also a smaller consciousness. Maybe I could get away with calling it eternal or transpersonal consciousness, especially if these terms do not call to mind a contrary, but are considered to include the opposites of both temporal and nontemporal, personal and nonpersonal. But I can't be sure that those terms won't call to mind an opposite. Therefore it's probably safer to be satisfied with the unadorned term, consciousness, even though we cannot define its precise meaning.

And there's another problem with this term, consciousness. Each of us believes we know exactly what it means, but actually it's very mysterious. However I can't help it; I don't have a better word so I feel I have to stick with it.

So I come down to the statement that the coniunctio means consciousness. To make it a little more problematic, however, I must add that consciousness is both cause and effect of the coniunctio. It must be stated in this paradoxical way because it is a product of both centers of the psyche, the ego and the Self. On the one hand, the efforts of the ego create the coniunctio but, on the other, fate decides, and the ego is a victim of a decision made "over [its] head or in defiance of [its] heart," as Jung puts it.[22]

One of the terms I mentioned for the coniunctio was *filius philosophorum,* the son of the philosophers. I think that's particularly significant, psychologically, because the alchemists called themselves philosophers. So what they mean by that term, *filius philosophorum,* is that the coniunctio is the son of the alchemist, and this would reflect the fact that it's created by the alchemist's efforts in the laboratory.

This is very important psychologically because it refers to the crucial role of the ego in the creation of consciousness. For instance, in one text the Philosophers' Stone says of itself:

> Then it was that I first knew my son /
> And we two came together as one.
> . . . . . . . . . . . . . . . .
> Therefore my son was also my father /
> . . . . . . . . . . . . . . . . [and]
> I bore the mother who gave me birth.[23]

---

[22] *Mysterium,* par. 778.

[23] "Psychology of the Transference," *Practice of Psychotherapy,* CW 16, par. 528. See below, pp. 101f., for further comments on this text.

These paradoxical statements mean that although the unconscious gives birth to the ego, "my son," yet it is the effort of the ego that impregnates the unconscious. Therefore the ego serves as a parent for the rebirth of the unconscious Self in a regenerate form.

Now I want to turn to something else. Embedded in the midst of this great book is a most extraordinary section. It extends from paragraph 186 to paragraph 211. How many of you would like to have the opportunity for a personal analytic hour with Jung? I think a lot of us would. I don't believe I'm overstating it by saying that this particular section of *Mysterium Coniunctionis* offers each person who is able to prepare sufficiently for it, the possibility of having just such an hour.

I'll tell you why. In this section Jung takes an obscure alchemical recipe and gives it a detailed psychological interpretation, taking the text as though it were a dream. To my knowledge, nowhere else in his work does he do anything like this.

I value this passage very highly because this particular alchemical text is really a collective dream. It's a dream any of us might have had, because it comes from such a level that it's of a general relevance, it's applicable to all of us. Therefore all that's required is that you become able to appreciate how this particular text is your dream, and then you take it to Jung and he interprets it for you. And, if you understand thoroughly the meaning of this dream—since I'm making rash statements tonight, I'll make another one—you will have had a complete analysis.

I'm going first to read you the text of the dream, the alchemical text that Jung works with, and don't be alarmed at its confusion. I'll hope to make it clearer as I proceed. Here it is:

> If thou knowest how to moisten this dry earth with its own water, thou wilt loosen the pores of the earth, and this thief from outside will be cast out with the workers of wickedness, and the water, by an admixture of the true Sulphur, will be cleansed from the leprous filth and from the superfluous dropsical fluid, and thou wilt have in thy power the fount of the Knight of Treviso, whose waters are rightfully dedicated to the maiden Diana. Worthless is this thief, armed with the malignity of arsenic, from whom the winged youth fleeth, shuddering. And though the central water is his bride, yet dare he not display his most ardent love towards her, because of the snares of the thief, whose machinations are in truth unavoidable. Here may Diana be propitious to thee, who knoweth how to tame wild beasts, and whose twin doves will temper the malignity of the air with their wings, so that the youth easily entereth in through the pores, and instantly shaketh the foundations of the earth, and raises up a dark cloud. But thou wilt lead the waters up even to the

brightness of the moon, and the darkness that was upon the face of the deep shall be scattered by the spirit moving over the waters. Thus by God's command shall the Light appear.[24]

Again, don't be alarmed, because this can be translated into something easier to grasp. Here's how I would translate it:

There is a fountain whose water is polluted. A winged youth burns with love for this fountain and, actually, the fountain is meant to be his bride. But, there is an evil thief who is the polluter of the fountain, and he prevents the approach of the winged youth. Then, with the help of Diana, the youth enters the pores of the earth adjacent to the fountain, and this union causes an earthquake and raises up a dark cloud.

When things have settled, the waters of the fountain have been purified and the world has been created (as in the first chapter of Genesis, where the spirit of God moved on the face of the waters and the darkness vanished and light appeared).

This image depicts the coniunctio and the opposites that come together are the fountain and the winged youth. They also represent other pairs of opposites: they represent water and fire, for instance, mercury and sulphur, and moon and sun. But, before that union can take place, the evil thief must be dealt with. And the thief, Jung says, "personifies a kind of self-robbery" due to collective thinking.[25] In the text, the thief is characterized as crude Sulphur in contrast with true Sulphur.

Now, what is sulphur? What does it mean psychologically? Jung has a wonderful passage, extending for many pages in *Mysterium,* on the symbolism of sulphur. He concludes with these words:

Sulphur represents the active substance of the sun or, in psychological language, the *motive factor in consciousness:* on the one hand the will . . . and on the other hand compulsion, an involuntary motivation or impulse ranging from mere interest to possession proper. The unconscious dynamism would correspond to sulphur, for compulsion is the great mystery of human life. It is the thwarting of our conscious will and of our reason by an inflammable element within us, appearing now as a consuming fire and now as life-giving warmth.[26]

To condense that still further, I'd say that sulphur is desirousness. It is the fire of libido, which is life energy itself. It's the energy created by the

---

[24] *Mysterium,* par. 186.

[25] Ibid., par. 194.

[26] Ibid., par. 151.

dynamo of the opposites.

But the alchemical text tells us there are two sulphurs: a crude or vulgar sulphur and a true or philosophical sulphur, and it's only the true sulphur that can enter into the coniunctio.

Psychologically, this would refer to ego-centered desirousness as contrasted with Self-centered desirousness. Ego-centered desirousness is of an unconscious, infantile nature that demands to have what it wants when it wants it, whereas desirousness that's centered in the Self is regenerate or

Sulphur as sun and Mercurius as moon bridging the river of eternal water (Barchusen, Elementa chemiae, 1718)

transformed desire which the ego serves as a religious duty. It is desire whose nature has been transformed by consciousness.

Unregenerate desirousness is evil, and you can demonstrate that evil nature very readily. All you have to do, when confronted in yourself or others with the crude sulphur, with the unregenerate desirousness, is to frustrate it, deny it, and you'll see immediately that it turns vicious. It turns demanding. It turns tyrannical, power-ridden. It immediately demonstrates its true nature when it's denied fulfillment, and that's not the case with the regenerate desirousness.

There's a wonderful passage in Jung's *Visions Seminars* where he tells us how to deal with desirousness. I want to read it to you:

> In this transformation it is essential to take objects away from those animus or anima devils. They only become concerned with objects when you allow yourself to be self-indulgent. *Concupiscentia* is the term for that in the church .... The fire of desirousness is the element that must be fought against in Brahmanism, in Buddhism, in Tantrism, in Manicheanism, in Christianity. It is also important in psychology.
>
> When you indulge in desirousness, whether your desire turns toward heaven or hell, you give the animus or the anima an object; then it comes out in the world instead of staying inside in its place.... But if you can say: Yes, I desire it and I shall try to get it but I do not have to have it, if I decide to renounce, I can renounce it; then there is no chance for the animus or anima. Otherwise you are governed by your desires, you are possessed. ...
>
> ... But if you have put your animus or anima into a bottle you are free of possession, even though you may be having a bad time inside, because when your devil has a bad time you have a bad time.... Of course he will rumble around in your entrails, but after a while you will see that it was right [to bottle him up]. You will slowly become quiet and change. Then you will discover that there is a stone growing in the bottle .... Insofar as self-control, or non-indulgence, has become a habit, it is a stone. ... When that attitude becomes a *fait accompli,* the stone will be a diamond.[27]

And the diamond is another image for the coniunctio.

Jung gives us further advice of the same nature in his interpretation of our *Mysterium* text. It is a very important passage that I return to time and time again, and I hope you will too. Remember, this is what takes place in your personal analytic hour with Jung—he's talking directly to you:

> You are so sterile because, without your knowledge, something like an evil spirit has stopped up the source of your fantasy, the fountain of your soul. The enemy is your own crude sulphur, which burns you with the hellish fire of desirousness, or *concupiscentia.* You would like to make gold because "poverty is the greatest plague, wealth the highest good." You wish to have results that flatter your pride, you expect something useful, but there can be no question of that as you have realized with a shock. Because of this you no longer even *want* to be fruitful, as it would only be for Cod's sake but unfortunately not for your own. ...
>
> Therefore away with your crude and vulgar desirousness, which childishly and shortsightedly sees only goals within its own narrow horizon. ...

---

[27] *The Visions Seminars,* vol. 1, p. 239-240.

Therefore bethink you for once, . . . and consider: What is behind all this desirousness? A thirsting for the eternal . . . . The more you cling to that which all the world desires, the more you are Everyman, who has not yet discovered himself and stumbles through the world like a blind man leading the blind with somnambulistic certainty into the ditch. Everyman is always a multitude. Cleanse your interest of that collective sulphur which clings to all like a leprosy. For desire only burns in order to burn itself out, and in and from this fire arises the true living spirit which generates life according to its own laws . . . . This means burning in your own fire and not being like a comet or a flashing beacon, showing others the right way but not knowing it yourself. The unconscious demands your interest for its own sake and wants to be accepted for what it is. Once the existence of this opposite is accepted, the ego can and should come to terms with its demands. Unless the content given you by the unconscious is acknowledged, its compensatory effect is not only nullified but actually changes into its opposite, as it then tries to realize itself literally and concretely.[28]

I want to underscore that remarkable statement: "What is behind all this desirousness? A thirsting for the eternal." Jung expresses the same idea in *Memories, Dreams, Reflections:*

The decisive question for man is: Is he related to something infinite or not? That is the telling question of his life. Only if we know that the thing which truly matters is the infinite can we avoid fixing our interest upon futilities, and upon all kinds of goals which are not of real importance. . . . If we understand and feel that here in this life we already have a link with the infinite, desires and attitude change.[29]

Now remember we're still talking about this alchemical text, the winged youth and the fountain of Diana. With the purification of desirousness, this youth can now penetrate the pores of the earth and unite with the waters. And as this happens, an earthquake occurs and there's the raising up of a dark cloud. This is an allusion to the darkness and earthquake that accompanied the death of Christ on the cross. And here's another wonderful statement Jung makes about that image. He says it tells us that "the widening of consciousness is at first upheaval and darkness, then a broadening out of man to the whole man."[30]

I hope you'll read the whole thing yourself. Jung goes into considerably more detail. But I'll conclude with just a few more words.

The world is torn asunder by the strife between the opposites, what Jung

[28] *Mysterium,* pars. 191-192.

[29] *Memories, Dreams, Reflections,* p. 325.

[30] *Mysterium,* par. 209.

calls "the wretched isms." As Emerson says: "All men plume themselves on the improvement of society, and no man improves."[31] And as Jung puts it in "The Undiscovered Self":

> If the individual is not truly regenerated in spirit, society cannot be either, for society is the sum total of individuals in need of redemption.[32]

Later in that same essay he makes some other important remarks:

> If only a world-wide consciousness could arise that all division and all fission are due to the splitting of opposites in the psyche, then we should know where to begin.[33]

> What does lie within our reach, however, is the change in individuals who have, or create for themselves, an opportunity to influence others of like mind. I do not mean by persuading or preaching—I am thinking, rather, of the well-known fact that anyone who has insight into his own actions, and has thus found access to the unconscious, involuntarily exercises an influence on his environment.[34]

These individuals with insight into their own actions are those who have, to a greater or lesser extent, experienced the coniunctio. They are carriers of the opposites. If society is to be redeemed, I think it will be done through the cumulative effect of such individuals. And when enough individuals carry the consciousness of wholeness, the world itself will become whole.

In antiquity, drama was part of a religious ceremony in the worship of Dionysus. When a play was bad, it was greeted with the remark, "That has nothing to do with Dionysus." My thought is that the future may generate new standards of thought and action derived from a new myth, and that those new standards will be based on the coniunctio as the highest good. From that standpoint, the profoundest criticism will be: "It has nothing to do with the coniunctio."

According to this Jungian myth, the highest measure of an individual's worth will be that he or she has a consciousness that is able to carry the opposites. Such people will not pollute the psychic atmosphere by projecting their shadow onto others, but rather will carry their own burden of darkness.

Jung puts it very beautifully in paragraph 512 of *Mysterium Coniunc-*

---

[31] "Self Reliance," in *Selected Writings,* p. 166.

[32] *Civilization in Transition,* CW 10, par. 536.

[33] Ibid., par. 575.

[34] Ibid., par. 583.

*tionis,* with which I will close. He says:

> If the projected conflict is to be healed, it must return into the psyche of the
> individual, where it had its unconscious beginnings. He must celebrate a Last
> Supper with himself, and eat his own flesh and drink his own blood; which
> means that he must recognize and accept the other in himself. . . . Is this
> perhaps the meaning of Christ's teaching, that each must bear his own cross?
> For if you have to endure yourself, how will you be able to rend others also?

*

## Discussion

*Question:* Is the coniunctio a once-and-for-all experience, or is it a goal that
one must work toward but that somehow always remains beyond one's
grasp?

Yes. Definitely. It is not a once-and-for-all experience, certainly not. I
see it as a cyclic phenomenon. Tomorrow I'm going to be talking about the
*Rosarium* pictures, a sequence of ten pictures describing different phases of
the coniunctio process, and I see that sequence of ten stages in a circular
pattern, a cycle.

One goes through that cycle many times, sometimes in small ways and
sometimes in large ways. There may be only one or two occasions in one's
life when one has the major encounter, the really earth-shaking one, but
smaller versions of the same process are going on all the time and creating
progressive increments of consciousness.

*Question:* What can one do to disengage when one becomes the screen
for a negative or positive projection? How does one avoid getting drawn
into the archetypal battle?

Jung goes into this matter very specifically in his lengthy introduction to
"The Psychology of the Transference,"[35] before he begins his commentary
on the *Rosarium* pictures. He discusses how it comes up in the analytic
process as the transference and countertransference, which is just what this
question is concerned with. Transference and countertransference are not
confined to the analytic relationship, of course. They happen everywhere in
life all the time. And it really is a very sizable issue—how to disengage
when one becomes entangled in projections that are felt to be coming from
the other person.

---

[35] *The Practice of Psychotherapy,* CW 16.

Here's one very important practical suggestion: in order to carry another person's projection, one has to offer a hook for it. No hook, no projection. If one has no tendency whatsoever to be what is projected, the projection falls off. It doesn't have anything to hold on to. So the thing to do if one is the recipient of a disagreeable projection, is to scrutinize oneself in search of hooks. You start by giving yourself the benefit of the doubt: "No, I'm not as much of what that person thinks I am, but I must be it to some extent; there must be some hook there or it wouldn't hold. And let me work on that hook." If you do that diligently, it can be very helpful.

*Question:* Is there a need for women to approach this coniunctio process differently from men?

To my knowledge, no. What I'm talking about is of such a general nature that it's universally applicable, and whatever variations there might be can be worked out subsequently. But as I see it, what I'm referring to has no significant difference between men and women.

*Question:* You and the Jung passages you quoted say that desirousness is evil, a devil that needs to be bottled up. Would you please discuss the difference between this and repression.

That's an important question, because the kind of recommendation Jung gives could sound like repression, but it's not. The critical thing, of course, is whether or not it's a conscious operation. Repression disposes of a disagreeable issue by rendering it unconscious, splitting it off to a greater or lesser extent, whereas Jung's advice is to seal it in the vessel—to use the alchemical image—and let it heat there. That's totally different from repression.

*Question:* What about the union of the same—not the union of the opposites, but union of the same?

Union of the same is a prelude to union of the opposites, because union of the same means that whatever the same is, it has not achieved its full reality as yet and needs to be united with more of its own stuff. And when that is completed, it can go on to union with the opposite.

*Question:* Can you be more specific regarding practical suggestions for incorporating the shadow? Perhaps a specific example of what one goes through after recognizing a portion of one's psyche in someone one hates? I mean, how to deal with guilt, rejection, self-hate, the need to be rational.

Well, let's see. Practical suggestions for incorporating the shadow. The first step is a crucial one, namely the ability to notice that what one is doing may be subject to question. Initially, one is in a state of innocence; one has whatever reactions one has; one loves this and hates that, and no question comes up as to whether it's suitable or not. Once that question comes up in a decisive way, one is no longer innocent; then one becomes troubled. I might hate such and such because it's so bad, but I don't feel very good when I'm hating either. In fact I feel kind of bad when I'm hating, so maybe I'm even being bad in the act of hating and maybe that's not so different from the badness that I hate in the other person.

As those reflections start to come, then, as Jung put it, we start eating our own flesh and drinking our own blood. I don't know how to be more specific, other than to suggest doing that at every opportunity.

*Question:* If the coniunctio gives birth to consciousness, what about its opposite, unconsciousness?

Yes, it does that too. It's an example of the fact that one can scarcely talk about psychological matters in any specific way without constellating the opposite of what one is talking about. And then you can get hopelessly tangled up.

The way the coniunctio can give birth to unconsciousness is that when it erupts in full power and encounters the ego, it can bowl the ego over and take possession of it. And then the very sense of insight and revelation and splendid awareness of vast dimensions turns into its opposite—an inflation. So in the very moment when one is having a great revelation, one is being an idiot by identifying with it. So, yes, in that sense the coniunctio gives birth to unconsciousness as well as consciousness.

*Question:* Would you elaborate on the value of guilt?

One of the major operations of the alchemical process is one called mortificatio.[36] That's a symbolic image for the material in the flask being subjected to killing, to putrefaction, to dismemberment, to all that's implied by that ugly term, mortification. Subjecting the material to death, in it's literal usage. This is a major image of the alchemical process.

The alchemists thought they were applying these operations to the material in the flask, but we know that that operation goes on in the psyche. And

---

[36] See below, pp. 68ff; also Edinger, *Anatomy,* chap. 6.

that was what I meant when I spoke of the necessity of the experience of defeat for full individuation. You can't have the experience of the opposites and their resolution without the experience of defeat, which is associated with mortificatio symbolism.

Now one can see perverse manifestations of that archetype when individuals as self-flagellators go in search of the experience. That's all wrong. That does not achieve its aim. It's not an operation that the ego can impose on itself, and it's a morbid perversity when it operates that way. But when the unconscious, when fate, when objective circumstances confront one with the experience of humiliation and defeat and even threat of literal death, it's just at those times that the most important psychological developments often take place.

One alchemical statement says that death is the conception of the Philosophers' Stone. The death of the ego, or the ego experiencing itself as dying, is very often the prelude to the birth of awareness of the Self. Jung makes the profound statement in *Mysterium* that "the experience of the self is always a defeat for the ego."[37] That's because an encounter with the greater thing always has a wounding and damaging effect, initially, on the lesser thing. And the experience of guilt belongs to this whole phenomenon of defeat and inadequacy and wounding.

*Question:* How does one deal effectively, realistically, responsibly, with political issues such as the threat of nuclear war, involvement in Central America and so on, while being aware of and containing the opposites within?

That's a very good question, and it's very difficult. I would remind you of Emerson's remark: "All men plume themselves on the improvement of society, and no man improves."[38] There certainly are individuals whose life work and destiny require them to deal with political realities. That's the arena in which they live out their life. And each of us, trying to be as conscious as possible, must ask ourselves what our proper life arena is. If we decide that our life arena is politics, then we will be obliged to prepare ourselves to function effectively in that arena and live out our life there.

If, however, one's life arena is something else and yet one is in great distress at what is going on in the world, and one thinks, "Oh I ought to do

---

[37] *Mysterium ,* par. 778.

[38] See above, p. 25, note 31.

something about it," my suggestion would be to think twice. Jung's conviction is that the most effective way to redeem or transform the world is first of all to transform the little piece of it that is oneself. And until that has been thoroughly accomplished, my thought would be that one isn't entitled to attempt the transformation of the outer world—unless, of course, one's work arena happens to be there.

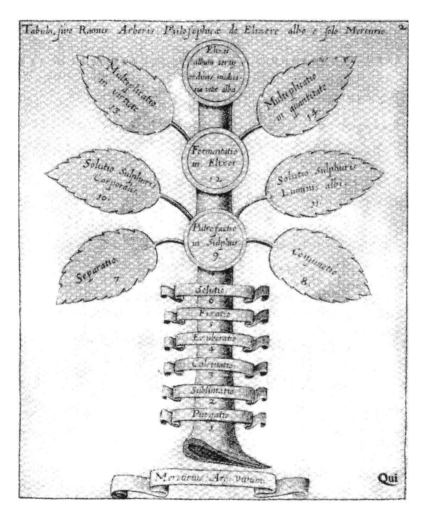

Alchemical operations in the form of the philosophical tree
*(Mutus liber,* 1677)

The alchemist and his assistant kneel by the furnace with the sealed phial inside.
Above them, two angels hold the same phial, containing Sol and Luna,
the spiritual equivalents of the two adepts.
*(Mutus liber,* 1677)

# 2

# A Psychological Interpretation
## of the *Rosarium* Pictures

Today we are going to talk about a series of ten pictures from the alchemical text *Rosarium philosophorum.* Jung thought so much of this series that he built one of his major works, "The Psychology of the Transference," around it. As he tells us in the introduction to *Mysterium Coniunctionis,* "The Psychology of the Transference" is part of the same enterprise as *Mysterium*, but in order not to overburden that big work he decided to put it out separately.[39]

My initial reaction to this material was, "My God, why did Jung choose something as obscure as the *Rosarium philosophorum* to talk about the transference?" But through the years, as I've worked with this material and reflected on it, it has dawned on me more and more that these pictures are magical. It's also clear that they derive from an original experience. Whoever was responsible for these pictures—and that person is lost in the anonymous mists of alchemy—had had the experience and was speaking out of it.

The *Rosarium* pictures are well worth the effort and attention one must pour into them in order to bring them into relation to the modern mind. My hope is that for many of you they will take on a meaning that will help you relate to the deeper psychological experiences you have had and shall have, and that they will be a permanent addition to your consciousness.

To start with, let's go over all ten of them very quickly. I've labeled each picture with a term of my own to help fix it in consciousness. I'll give you an overview of those now and then we'll go on to examine each picture in detail.

---

[39] "The Psychology of the Transference" was first published in book form as *Dies Psychologie der Übertragung* (Zurich, 1946). In the English edition of Jung's *Collected Works* it is now included in *The Practice of Psychotherapy,* CW 16. The woodcuts reproduced there, and here, are from the Frankfurt first edition of *Rosarium philosophorum* (1550).

**Picture 1**
**The Mandala Fountain**

**Picture 2**
**Emergence of the Opposites**

**Picture 3**
**Stripped for Action**

**Picture 4**
**Descent into the Bath**

**Picture 5**
**Union, Manifestation of the Mystery**

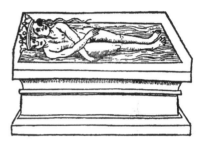

**Picture 6**
**In the Tomb**

**Picture 7**
**Separation of Soul and Body**

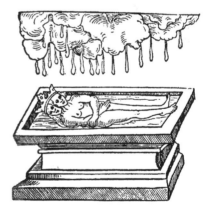

**Picture 8**
**Gideon's Dew Drips from the Cloud**

**Picture 9**
**Reunion of Soul and Body**

**Picture 10**
**Resurrection of the United Eternal Body**

1. The Mandala Fountain, representing the *prima materia*
2. The Emergence of the Opposites
3. Stripped for Action
4. Descent into the Bath
5. Union, the manifestation of the Mystery
6. In the Tomb
7. Separation of Soul and Body
8. Gideon's Dew Drips from the Cloud
9. Reunion of Soul and Body
10. Resurrection of the United Eternal Body

Now although I've presented these in a linear fashion, I think it is better to think of them as arranged in a circle representing a cycle, as shown in diagram 1. When arranged that way you can think of them as a sequence of psychological events that can repeat itself over and over, rather than as a single, isolated occurrence.

Another advantage to this arrangement is that one can perceive the parallels this series has with other cycles. Some of you will remember our seminars on the Christian archetype in past years.[40] There I arranged the

---

[40] See Edinger, *The Christian Archetype: A Jungian Commentary on the Life of Christ.*

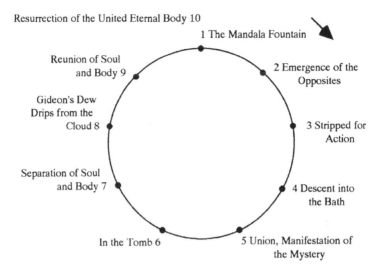

**Diagram 1. The *Rosarium* cycle**

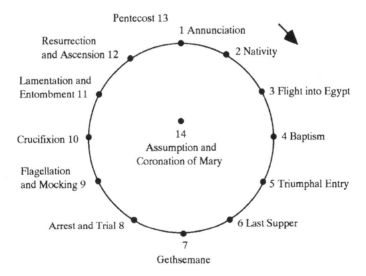

**Diagram 2. The Incarnation Cycle**

various nodal points in the life of Christ in the form of a cycle, shown in diagram 2. If you compare this with the *Rosarium* cycle, you can see the similarities once you've grasped their underlying psychological references.

Let me spell out the parallels I see between the cycle of the Christian archetype and the cycle of the *Rosarium* pictures:

Picture 2, Emergence of the Opposites, is analogous to Annunciation.

Picture 3, Stripped for Action, is analogous to the Nativity.

Picture 4, Descent into the Bath, is analogous to Christ's baptism.

Picture 5, Union, is analogous to the Crucifixion.

Pictures 6 to 8, In the Tomb, Separation of Soul and Body, and Gid-eon's Dew, correspond to the Crucifixion, Lamentation and Entombment of Christ.

Pictures 9 and 10, Reunion of Soul and Body, and Resurrection of the United Eternal Body, correspond to the Resurrection and Ascension.

There's another analogous cycle. Gilbert Murray, the great classical scholar (1866-1957), has given us a very valuable description of the cyclic religious drama underlying classic Greek tragedy.[41] He sees that basic cycle, the origin of tragic drama, as a ritual reenactment of the death and rebirth of the Year Spirit. This ritual reenactment had four chief features or phases:

1. The protagonist hero who is Dionysus, the personification of the Year Spirit, meets an antagonist. He meets an embodiment of evil and the opposites are constellated. A contest, called the *Agon* in Greek, ensues between the protagonist and the antagonist. That's the first phase.

2. It leads to a passion or suffering and defeat of Dionysus, the Year Spirit. That's the *Pathos.*

3. This is then followed by a lamentation, the *Threnos,* on the part of the chorus, the observers of the drama.

4. Then a miraculous enantiodromia takes place and the god remanifests; he resurrects, reappears on another level, and that's called the *Theophany.*

Again I've put that sequence in a circle (diagram 3) in order to compare it with the others. I think you'll see as we go along that it closely parallels the *Rosarium* pictures. I think these parallels are inevitable because these cycles all derive from the same basic archetype.

---

[41] "Excursus on the Ritual Forms Preserved in Greek Tragedy," pp. 343f.

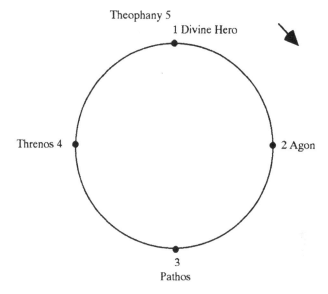

**Diagram 3**
**The death and rebirth of the Year Spirit**

The pattern of the *Rosarium* pictures represents symbolically the stages of a dynamic process in the objective psyche. I must remind you that the pictures we're looking at today are alchemical pictures, and they are meant to illustrate events going on in the alchemical flask. You might forget that because they're not shown enclosed in the flask. But that's what they're meant to represent. They express events taking place within a vessel, within a containing entity.

In my attempt to understand these matters psychologically, I'm going to follow a course somewhat different from Jung's. There's no point in my just repeating what he has to say, but I urge you to read that for yourself. I'm going to suggest various other ways to look at the pictures. It's not a matter of either/or but of examining various facets. As with all major symbolic images they shimmer with a multitude of meanings and you can probably think of some more yourself if you're so inclined. For my purposes, I'm going to consider this series of pictures as representing three different psychological contexts.

1. The first one, a process going on within the individual psyche. In that

case, the vessel containing the process would be a single individual.

2. A second way of seeing it psychologically is as a process going on between two people. In that case the containing vessel would be the relationship; it would reside with the pair.

3. A third way of seeing it is that it represents a psychological process going on within a group or community. In that case it's a collective process, not personal at all. The individuals who make up the group will just be the atoms, so to speak, of the larger collective drama.

The more familiar one becomes with alchemical symbolism, the more evident it is that the alchemical images apply to *everything;* they're operative everywhere. So if one is going to use the imagery for understanding a certain experience or phenomenon, one does need to define the vessel that a given alchemical process is taking place in. And the three most common vessels are the ones I've mentioned here: the individual psyche, a relationship between two people, or a process going on in a larger group.

Now let's examine the *Rosarium* pictures one by one.

### Picture 1. The Mandala Fountain

Here we have a picture of a fountain with a kind of flowerlike decoration on top of it. From it three pipes spout a fluid into a containing basin. It is surrounded by an approximately square structure with a two-headed serpent at the top, each head spouting a vapor.

That's a reference to an ancient idea that the four elements first derived from two vapors. Initially there were two vapors—a smoky vapor and a watery vapor. The smoky vapor divided into two, becoming earth and air, and the watery vapor divided into two, fire and water. You can see that the two vapors spit out by the serpent then generate four six-pointed stars, one in each of the four corners. Those signify the four elements: earth, air, fire, water. There is a fifth star in the center which signifies the quintessence or fifth entity, created by the unification of the four elements. And then on either side are the sun and moon.

This picture represents both the *prima materia* and the *ultima materia.* It's really outside the sequence. It belongs just as much at the end as at the beginning; it's alpha and omega, representing both ends of the process.

This is the so-called Mercurial Fountain, the fountain of Mercurius, and psychologically it would signify the foundation of the psyche prior to the birth of the ego.

In the earliest stages of development, in youth, the ego lives to a large

# ROSARIVM

Wyr findt der metall anfang vnd erfte natur /
Die kunft macht durch vns die höchfte tinctur.
Keyn brunn noch waffer ift meyn gleych/
Jch mach gefund arm vnd reych.
Vnd bin doch jßund gyftig vnd ödtlich.

**Succus**

*We are the metals' first nature and only source /*
*The highest tincture of the Art is made through us.*
*No fountain and no water has my like /*
*I make both rich and poor both whole and sick.*
*For healthful can I be and poisonous.*

Picture 1
The Mandala Fountain

extent in identification with what this picture symbolizes. The fountain spurts out its life-giving fluids without much trouble because there's no reflection yet. But in later life, in the process of individuation, the ego is obliged to relate to what this picture represents and live it out consciously.

I would draw to your attention the fact that the images are cosmic (stars, sun and moon), inorganic (represented by the four elements and the vapors) and reptilian. This is what the foundation of the human psyche is. It's of that nature; there's nothing human about it. It isn't even mammalian; it doesn't even have the degree of connection with us that warm blood would give.

An image such as this is very often an end product of analysis. Usually it doesn't show up at the beginning at all except in cases where the need is to analyze one out of the unconscious rather than into it.

I'd also draw your attention to how much is condensed into this picture. For instance, built into it is the symbolic sequence 1, 2, 3, 4. There's one fountain in the center but just above it are two representations of duality: the son and the moon on the one hand, and the two-headed serpent on the other. The number three is built into the picture by the three spouts in the fountain. They are labeled "virgin's milk," "vinegar of the fountain" and "water of life." These are various synonyms for the elixir, the *aqua permanens,* the liquid version of the Philosophers' Stone. The quaternity is represented by the four stars in the corners symbolizing the four elements. Even the number five is alluded to by the fifth star.

Now this sequence of 1, 2, 3, 4, is the so-called axiom of Maria. It's very important for Jung so when I was thinking about this I said to myself, let's just see how often he refers to it. So I looked it up in the index to the *Collected Works* and found thirty-six references to the axiom of Maria.

Maria Prophetissa, Maria the Jewess, was a famous early alchemist; she was a kind of ancestress of the alchemists. Her axiom is this: "One becomes two, two becomes three, and out of the third comes the one as the fourth."[42] And there's another version: "One and it is two; and two and it is three; and three and it is four; and four and it is three; and three and it is two, and two and it is one."[43]

You know, the more one reflects on the first simple integers the more mysterious and significant they become. The axiom of Maria corresponds to the ancient Pythagorean tetractys which was represented like this:

---

[42] *Psychology and Alchemy,* CW 12, par. 209.
[43] Ibid., par. 210, note 86.

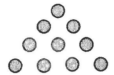

The brotherhood of Pythagoreans worshipped the tetractys as their most sacred emblem. They were living at a time when numbers were just being discovered. The numinosity of numbers and the relation between numbers gripped these early discoverers profoundly; they were in such close touch with the archetypal background of numbers that its sacred aura was immediately perceptible to them. We have to work very hard to get back into that state of mind, and in order to do so we must go down into the unconscious. Pythagorean philosophy still lives in our unconscious, and if we go down deeply enough then the numinosity of those original things starts to grip us also. This sort of thing is all built into this first picture. The alchemists still had some feeling for these qualities but we've very largely lost it.

Jung says somewhere that the first five simple integers, 1, 2, 3, 4, 5, are the basis of a whole cosmogony.[44] If we had more time I would run through this double axiom of Maria and show you how it represents the psychological development of both the first and second half of life. One becomes two, two becomes three, three becomes four; four becomes three, three becomes two, two becomes one. Down and back up again, from unity down to fourfold multiplicity and then back, in steps, up to unity.

That's a symbolic resumé of the first and second halves of life. I don't have time to go into it now but maybe that's sufficient for you to figure it out for yourselves.[45]

Now, as we go through each picture, I want to mention at least briefly how such images also come up in modern dreams. This first picture would correspond to mandala structures: the circle and the square, the fountain, the numbers, and especially the very common dream images referring to the theme of the three and the four. These are images that come up as unifying symbols in the analytic process, and although they're often an end product

---

[44] See *Memories, Dreams, Reflections,* pp. 310f.

[45] For a fuller discussion see Edinger, *The Mysterium Lectures,* lecture 23.

of a phase of development, they can sometimes come up early as foreshadowings of future integration.

## Picture 2. Emergence of the Opposites

Here we have a robed king and queen, each crowned. The king stands on the sun and the queen stands on the moon. They hold each other's left hand and in the right hand of each there are long-stemmed flowers which cross. Above them is a six-pointed star. Since this star is central we can assume it derives from that fifth quintessential star of the first picture. Below the star, a dove descends with another flower in its beak which crosses the two other crossed flower stems.

In the first picture we had a representation of the original unity, and now that unity has been split into two. The king and the queen face each other. There's a confrontation, and that confrontation takes place under the motivation of a third thing, the dove. So in comparison to Picture 1, this represents a separatio corresponding to the original act of creation that separated light from darkness. That's a very frequent theme of creation myths. In the beginning there was just a confused composite mixture of things and then a divine intervention caused a division, separating the earth from the sky. In this case it's the sun from the moon.[46]

The creative act of separatio means consciousness has been born, and consciousness means human beings. Therefore in Picture 2 we have for the first time the presence of humanity. But they're not quite ordinary human beings, they're not persons yet. From the way they're represented it's clear they are archetypal entities rather than individuals. That's indicated in two ways: first of all, they're standing on the sun and the moon. Secondly they are royalty, represented by the crowns and robes. One might say the fact that they're standing on the sun and the moon indicates that they represent Sol and Luna as reflected in human consciousness. Also we should understand Sol and Luna, in light of general alchemical symbolism, to refer to all the pairs of opposites.

The dove is a very interesting phenomenon here—it's clearly the instigator of the whole ensuing drama. I see it as playing something of the same role as the serpent played in the Garden of Eden. I've already mentioned that the Annunciation parallels this picture; the dove of the Holy

---

[46] See Edinger, *Anatomy,* chap. 7, "Separatio."

# PHILOSOPHORVM.

Nota bene: In arte noſtri magiſterij nihil eſt Secretum
celatū à Philoſophis excepto ſecreto artis, quod artis
non licet cuiquam reuelare, quod ſi fieret ille ma
lediceretur , & indignationem domini incur⸗
reret, & apoplexia moreretur. Quare om⸗
nis error in arte exiſtit , ex eo, quod debitam

C ij

**Picture 2**
**Emergence of the Opposites**

*The Annunciation,* showing two angelic presences
(Giovanni di Paolo, Sienese, ca. 1445. Nat. Gallery of Art, Washington, DC)

Ghost was involved there. And, as those of you who heard me talk on the symbolism of the Annunciation will remember, that symbolism has definite analogies to the temptation in the Garden of Eden.[47] The angelic presences (seen in the di Paolo painting above) at the Annunciation and in the Garden of Eden are two manifestations of the same psychological reality. Here it is again in Picture 2.

The dove has two major symbolic references: the Holy Ghost is one, and the dove of Aphrodite is the other. So symbolically these two different aspects are put together into one paradoxical image. Now that's a union of opposites in itself. The promptings of Aphrodite and the promptings of the Holy Ghost usually aren't thought of as identical!

Psychologically this would mean that the beginning of the coniunctio is

---

[47] See Edinger, *The Christian Archetype,* pp. 23ff.

set off by an ardent desire—Aphrodite is the mother of desires—and this desire is at the same time an Annunciation of the Holy Ghost. That the dove descends from the star indicates that it's a messenger from the transpersonal or cosmic Self.

*The Annunciation,* showing the Holy Ghost descending as a dove
(From *The Belles Heures of Jean, Duke of Berry.* The Cloisters,
Metropolitan Museum of Art.)

You see desire impels us toward an object in anticipation of pleasure, whereas an annunciation is an assignment of a difficult task—it's an opus. Those two are actually the same thing, and the way one experiences either depends on the level of psychological development.

In youth we follow our desires with relative abandon until experience teaches us to know better. But in the course of individuation, we learn that to follow one's libido consciously becomes a heavy task, an opus. And in this picture these two aspects of the relation of the ego to transpersonal libido are united in the single image of the dove. You might say it's a union of work and play.

You remember I said that there were three ways we can take these pictures: as a process within the individual, as process within a relationship between two people, or as a process within a collectivity.

It's very interesting to me that in the ancient Greek grammar there were three numbers. No wonder the teaching of ancient Greek has gone out of fashion! Not only are there singular and plural forms to learn, you also have dual forms. So there's single, dual and plural. If the reference is to one person you use the singular form; if it is to two people you use a dual form; and if it's to more than two—three or many—you use the plural. The way language crystallizes out in early development is an expression of the phenomenology of the psyche. So this Greek grammatical structure is an example of the same thing I'm doing here—interpreting these pictures in three modes, single, dual and plural. One, you're alone, two's company, three's a crowd.

I should remind you of another feature. The activation of libido that the dove represents may be either positive or negative, an attraction or a hatred. Enmity promotes coniunctio just as well, maybe even better, than love does. They are two sides of the same phenomenon, which is illustrated in Greek mythology by the fact that Ares, the god of war, and Aphrodite, the god of love, were lovers.

Let's consider how we might understand Picture 2 from the three different standpoints. As a process within the individual (this is not completely accurate psychologically, as these things are very fluid and variable), one way of thinking of it that will be partially true, at least sometimes, is that the male figure represents a man's ego and the female figure represents a woman's ego. I don't recommend identifying with those figures as a psychological process, but the fact is that we do. We fall into such identifications and then discover our mistake retrospectively and have to alter our ideas.[48]

With that idea in mind, from the individual standpoint such a picture could be saying something like this: the ego, having been goaded by Aphrodite and the Holy Ghost, is gripped by an intense affective urgency, either desire or hatred for something that derives from the anima or animus. The anima and animus are the personifications of our passionate desires because they're the gateway to the unconscious. Those figures will say, "Go for that," or, "Oh, that's terrible!" From this standpoint, Picture 2 would represent the initial phase of that goading by an affect of positive or negative desirousness. That would be the individual mode.

Considered as a relationship between two people, we could see it as a picture of a person being gripped by a passion of love or hate for another person. It's the initial move to touch, either to incorporate or destroy, that person who has aroused the affective intensity. You know very often that move toward another in so-called love actually has as its basis a desire to incorporate, take over, consume, swallow.

In the third way of seeing it, as a process within a social collective, the picture would represent two groups or factions that are motivated to confront each other. Such an event is almost always in enmity. You don't get a lot of loving connections between two groups within a single collective. So the initial encounter will be with the intention to destroy. Nonetheless this desire to destroy the opponent, the other, derives from an unconscious coniunctio urge.

I'm reminded of a bird that keeps showing up outside my window. It can see its reflection in the window and it can't leave it alone. It has to attack that reflection and its persistence is just astonishing. This has been going on for weeks! It cannot stand the presence of a second, and I think of this picture. But its behavior does derive from a coniunctio image: the urge to annihilate the second is a desire to reestablish unity.

I understand all empire-building, for instance, as deriving from the coniunctio urge. It's misplaced because it's ego-centered, but I think that's what gave Alexander the Great his impetus. He had a vision—a very premature one—of one world. And although it was acted out in identification with the ego, I'm convinced he was serving an archetypal principle.

This image comes up often in dreams. Two figures meet in a dream and

---

[48] See "Psychology of the Transference," *Practice of Psychotherapy,* CW 16, par. 469.

have some superficial initial encounters. Meetings of the ego and the shadow, for example, or sometimes of ego and anima or animus, or the meeting of two non-ego figures. But initial meetings happen all the time.

### Picture 3. Stripped for Action

We have the same two crowned figures standing on the sun and the moon and now their clothing is removed. The nature of their connection is also different. No longer are they holding left hands which signifies an unconscious connection. Instead, they are connected by the two flowers they mutually hold. The dove is still above with its additional flower crossing the other flowers. The star is missing and is replaced by its earthly embodiment, the sixfold star-flower which connects the two figures.

I think the flowers are primarily a reference to the erotic aspect of the motivating energy. In dreams, flowers generally point to two major ideas. When a single flower is emphasized, it's very often a mandala image since flowers are natural mandalas. The other idea is that flowers represent nature's capacity to attract. They are a manifestation of beauty, a lure. Presumably, from the teleological standpoint, that's why a plant generates flowers. They lure creatures to it that then serve its purposes. So psychologically considered, flowers would represent the beautiful bait that the unconscious holds out to the ego in order to lure it into the process of individuation. And one hopes that it's not a Venus Flytrap!

In this picture something new has been added—we have words. There were words in Picture 1 but they were sort of disembodied because there was no human consciousness to read them. Here each of the three figures is making a statement; we have language. This indicates that some significant changes have taken place in the encounter between these two opposites. On the scrolls, Sol is saying, "O Luna, let me be thy husband"; Luna says, "O Sol, I must submit to thee"; and the dove says, "The spirit is what unifies." Or in another version of this same picture the dove says, "The spirit is what vivifies."

Now as I mentioned, the left hands are no longer touching and the star has disappeared. As I understand it, the six-pointed star from the first two pictures has translated itself from the upper region to the space between the two figures. We now have a six-pointed figure held between the two figures and the dove. We had the beginnings of that six-pointed figure in

## PHILOSOPHORVM.

ſeipſis ſecundum ęqualitatē inſpiſſentur. Solus
enim calor tēperatus eſt humiditatis inſpiſſatiuus
et mixtionis perſectiuus, et non ſuper excedens.
N ã generatiões et procreationes rerū naturaliū
habent ſolū fieri per tēperatiſsimū calorē et ęqua
lē, vti eſt ſolus fimus equinus humidus et calidus.

**Picture 3**
**Stripped for Action**

Picture 2 but it wasn't yet completely joined because of the left-handed connection; the two figures weren't completely committed to the sixfold connection but now they are.

That suggests to me that the star, evidence of a transpersonal or cosmic dimension, has now been constellated in the relationship between Sol and Luna. This would correspond to the incarnation of deity, you see, the descent of the transpersonal content into the vessel of the relationship between these two figures. Or you could say that the *imago Dei* has fallen into the human realm.

I'm reminded of a couple of remarks of Jung's about this in "Answer to Job." He says:

> All opposites are of God, therefore man must bend to this burden; and in so doing he finds that God in his "oppositeness" has taken possession of him, incarnated himself in him. He becomes a vessel filled with divine conflict.[49]

> God acts out of the unconscious of man and forces him to harmonize and unite the opposing influences to which his mind is exposed from the unconscious.[50]

Let's consider what Picture 3 might mean in terms of the three modes of experience. First, within an individual, it would indicate that the opposites have been constellated and consciously engaged and that there's been a commitment to a particular enterprise. It might for instance be a commitment to pursue a desired object of some kind. It could be a person, it could be a car, it could be a profession, it could be anything big or little. It could represent a decision to engage the unconscious in some serious way, to go with it—these *Rosarium* images can apply to many different magnitudes of importance. But it will represent a commitment to follow an intense affect, either positive or negative. So in Picture 3 what was represented in Picture 2 as an unconscious urge becomes a conscious decision; the left-handed unconscious connection has ceased.

As a process going on within a relationship, it would suggest that the two participants have shed their personas and are now approaching each other with what Jung calls "the naked truth."[51] They're now mutually committed to pursuing the relationship—they're not just flirting as they were in Picture 2. Psychological intimacy is beginning and the third thing, the transpersonal

---

[49] *Psychology and Religion,* CW 11, par. 659.

[50] Ibid., par. 740.

[51] "Psychology of the Transference," *Practice of Psychotherapy,* CW 16, par. 452.

star, is constellated between them; it will live itself out in some way or other, for good or for ill.

Considered as a process within a collective, it would suggest that the two opposing factions have revealed their open enmity. Their personas of politeness have been stripped; they reveal their real attitude toward each other, and the prospect of war is escalating.

Images of this sort show up in dreams quite often. Nakedness in dreams is so common that it was even the basis of a commercial many years ago. "I dreamt I was in my Maidenform bra"—in some public place. Very often such an image refers to a faulty persona and indicates that the individual is heading for the bath waters unintentionally. One doesn't know what one is doing. Such dreams then remind the person, "Wait a minute, did you really intend to embark on this process or have you just blundered into it by mistake? If it's a blunder, get your clothes back on."

But at other times, the image of nakedness in dreams means psychological honesty. All pretenses have been stripped away and the process is going to proceed in earnest.

The red-and-white rose, the "golden flower" of alchemy,
as birthplace of the *filius philosophorum*
("Ripley Scrowle," 1588)

**Picture 4. Descent into the Bath**

Here we have a picture of a basin filled with water, a hexagonal basin, so the sixfold nature of the star and of the arrangement of the flowers is again duplicated on the lower level of the fountain. The naked crowned king and queen are sitting in the bath waters and again the dove is present.

The encounter has gone a step further and the two figures are now united not only by the flowers they hold but also by the medium of the water. They have begun a state of mutual solutio.

Solutio is a major alchemical image and it is likewise extremely important psychologically. The basic images that refer to this symbol system are such things as swimming in water, bathing, showering, maybe drowning, dissolution; but also baptism and rejuvenation through the process, through the ordeal by water. Solutio is an image of a descent into the unconscious that has the effect of dissolving the solid, ordered structure of the ego.[52] For the alchemist, the solutio meant the return of differentiated matter to its original undifferentiated state, to the *prima materia.* Water was thought of as the womb, and to enter the water, the solutio, was to return to the womb for rebirth. For instance in one text, the old king who submits to the solutio of drowning has this to say:

> Else I God's Kingdom cannot enter in:
> And therefore, that I may be Borne agen,
> I'le Humbled be into my Mother's Breast,
> Dissolve to my First Matter, and there rest.[53]

Well, the two figures are following that same recipe. Here is another alchemical recipe for solutio, from "The Secret Book of Artephius":

> Dissolve then sol and luna in our dissolving water, which is familiar and friendly, and the next in nature unto them, and as it were a womb, a mother, an original, the beginning and the end of their life. And that is the very reason why they are meliorated or amended in this water, because like nature rejoiceth in like nature. . . . Thus it behooves you to join consanguinity, or sameness of kind. . . . And because sol and luna have their origin from this water their mother; it is necessary therefore that they enter into it again, to wit, into their mother's womb, that they may be regenerate or born again, and made more healthy, more noble, and more strong.[54]

---

[52] See Edinger, *Anatomy,* chap. 3, "Solutio."

[53] *Mysterium Coniunctionis,* CW 14, par. 380.

[54] In *The Lives of the Alchemistical Philosophers*, pp. 145-146.

# ROSARIVM

corrūpitur, necp ex imperfecto penitus secundū artem aliquid fieri poteft. Ratio eft quia ars primas difpofitiones inducere non poteft, fed lapis nofter eft res media inter perfecta & imperfecta corpora, & quod natura ipfa incepit hoc per artem ad perfectionē deducitur. Si in ipfo Mercurio operari inceperis vbi natura reliquit imperfectum, inuenies in eo perfectionē et gaudebis.

Perfectum non alteratur, fed corrumpitur. Sed imperfectum bene alteratur, ergo corruptio vnius eft generatio alterius.

Speculum

**Picture 4**
**Descent into the Bath**

The image of the king and the queen in the bath, and the dissolution of Sol and Luna in this text, both refer to a chemical fact well known to the alchemists. For them, Sol and Luna, sun and moon, also refer to the metals gold and silver. The alchemists were gripped by the idea that these two metals representing the opposites had somehow to be united. And how do you get them together? Well, they discovered that one way to get them together was to amalgamate them with mercury; you'd then get an amalgam that is a mixture, a union, of gold and silver.

From the chemical standpoint that is what this picture represents: gold and silver being immersed in the mercurial fountain, in a bath of liquid mercury, in order to be dissolved. That's a chemical image of something that actually happens in the laboratory; but of course all the rich fantasy elaborations that the alchemists projected into it are an expression of the psychological process going on in the unconscious.

Picture 4 is an image of *participation mystique.* You see, as the recipe tells us, gold and silver were originally born out of the mother's womb, which corresponds to the mercurial fountain. Originally the opposites were separated and differentiated from the unconscious matrix, and now they are reversing direction and returning to that womb, merging again into their original state. And the recipe speaks of that in very sweet terms: "Our dissolving water, which is familiar and friendly." They are meliorated— softened—and rejoice as they dissolve; that's the idea.

Well, that's both true and not true psychologically because it depends on the level of ego development. We owe Erich Neumann a particular debt in this matter because he has elaborated in very fine fashion the various aspects of the phenomenon of fusion and merging with the Great Mother. In *The Origins and History of Consciousness* he makes the point that merging and dissolution in identification with the Great Mother, which is the same as merging in the mercurial fountain, is experienced in different ways depending on the level of development of the ego.[55]

For a quite immature ego, the opportunity to rid itself of the painful experience of having a separate existence is blissful. So it will plunge into the maternal fountain, lose its discriminated state, and experience it as bliss—a kind of ecstasy of oblivion. However, when the ego has developed to a somewhat greater extent, it then becomes aware of what a precious and precarious thing it is to have an autonomous existence. Then the

---

[55] *Origins,* part I, sections A and B.

Mercurius as *virgo* standing on the gold (Sol) and silver (Luna) fountain
(Thomas Aquinas, pseud.; *De alchimia,* 16th cent.)

threat of a return to that undifferentiated dissolved state is experienced as the horror of non-being. It's as though the mercurial fountain then takes on the aspect of the jaws of a devouring monster. An ego that has developed sufficiently to value its separate existence will flee from that experience in terror. Neumann elaborates this quite beautifully and that is what is at issue in Picture 4.

*Question:* The other way around too? With a mature ego, could you have a momentary blissful state, knowing you could come out of it?

The point is that none of us ever reaches that state of total maturity where a little element of "bliss" doesn't come in. In other words the psyche is a composite; it's not just one entity, it's a mixture of things, but in talking about the different stages we have to pretend they're more precisely separated than they are.

*Question:* This is such a happy picture, like a couple in a hot tub . . . but what about the opposite? You've been talking about the love aspect but there's also the animosity.

That's right. Let's consider these matters now from the standpoint of our three modes. First, thinking of the picture as representing a process within an individual, it would mean the plunge has been made into the unconscious. The individual has embraced the object of intense desire and the process of merging with it has begun. This will generally be experienced in positive terms; the negative aspect doesn't show up in consciousness until a couple of pictures later. We'll get to it but usually in the individual this is a pretty happy situation.

*Question:* As I understand it, sometimes it shows itself as love and sometimes as a battle. How does this stage represent itself in a dream—in individual, dual or collective form—when the situation involves animosity rather than love?

The same way. You see, identification with one's intense passion is a dissolution, either way.

Considering this as a process within a relationship, we could say that the movement of coming together has become irrevocable and the two people have begun a state of merging or mutual identification which amounts to *participation mystique.*

Alchemical images of solutio
*Above,* doing the washing; *below,* king and queen in the bath
(J.D. Mylius, *Philosophia reformata,* 1622)

Another important feature of intense personal relationships is well revealed by Picture 4. In this kind of configuration the innate Self that is potentially available to each individual is constellated in the vessel of the relationship. That's illustrated in this picture by the fact that the six-pointed star descends to the level of the six-pointed flower pattern and then descends all the way into the bath as the six-sided basin. This tells us that the transpersonal factor potentially available to each is being initially constellated in the relationship—it's not yet individualized. Each partner then has the experience of wholeness in the relationship, and that's a very valuable event.

It's not just a negative dissolution, you see, because the vessel that is containing the merged identification is a vessel representing the transpersonal entity. And this is a common phenomenon, you know, it can last for a lifetime. How many marriages do we see where the two partners make up two halves of a whole; the wholeness resides in the pair—not in either individual—and it works! And when one dies, the other dies very quickly because the containing vessel has been broken. That would be a picture of this state of affairs; it's as if the process stops at Picture 4.

The third possibility is that the picture is expressing a process within a collective. Now in that case, the two antagonistic factions have passed the point of no return and war has been declared. The meaning of the war, the meaning of the contest itself, will be the same hexagonal bath; it will have the same meaning as the relationship between two. This is how I understand Krishna's response to Arjuna in the Bhagavad-Gita. Arjuna is on the verge of a day of battle, but he doesn't want to fight. There are many of his kinsmen arrayed against him; he'd rather give up and says, "I don't want to fight against my kinsmen." Krishna, through the personification of his chariot driver, teaches him otherwise. Arjuna finally does battle.[56]

It's a difficult doctrine, very difficult, but the gist of it is, "You go in there and fight." We have to find a very large standpoint in order to understand that advice, and I think this imagery helps give us that standpoint. As long as the possibility of the coniunctio resides in the collective situation, then the individual serves the coniunctio aim by playing his or her part in the larger collective drama. That's how I understand it to be for Arjuna. After all, it was about 600 B.C. when that was written. In that case, then, if

---

[56] The relevant narrative in the Bhagavad-Gita takes place from the First Teaching, "Arjuna's Dejection," to the Third Teaching, "Discipline of Action."

destiny has put one in a time and place where the coniunctio is being manifested within a vessel of war, one must simply submit to it.

So far as this image in dreams is concerned, it is very common. All the various images that refer to solutio will be applicable. My whole chapter on solutio symbolism in *Anatomy of the Psyche* will apply to this picture. Basically it means getting wet with the unconscious, which has various possibilities. It is potentially auspicious and purifying, promoting renewal and rebirth. But it also has very alarming implications, in that one can undergo dissolution and drowning, death and dispersal. It often depends on whether one is looking at the issue in short-range or long-range terms.

In the short run, solutio images in dreams are very often ominous— floods, for instance, tidal waves. But over a lengthy dream series, one might look back at such dreams and see that they actually heralded major developmental steps; they were the harbinger of a death and rebirth experience. Of course, this is easier to perceive in retrospect than in prospect.

Image of solutio: the king sucked in by a whirlpool
(Michael Maier, *Atalanta Fugiens,* 1618)

## Picture 5. Union, Manifestation of the Mystery

Here we have a totally different set-up. The familiar images of the previous pictures are no longer visible. The two figures have submerged completely into the basin of the fountain and are under water, therefore not visible at all. But a little window has been cut through the wall of the basin so we can peek in and see what's going on under the surface. That's why I label it "Union, Manifestation of the Mystery." Because we really aren't supposed to be seeing this. It's a violation of the sacred mystery to be given this glimpse into the depths.

There's no dove; no star, of course, that was already gone; no longer a flower pattern. The sun and moon are still present; they've descended along with the figures, because the figures are personifications of the sun and moon, and they are in a state of intercourse.

So this pictures the consummation of the first half of the process. It reminds me of the Eleusinian mysteries. You know, we don't know for sure what happened in them. That secret was kept so well that we can't be certain of what the initiates experienced. But we have reason to believe that at the high point of the greater Eleusinian mysteries the priest and priestess descended into the depths and celebrated a sacred *heiros gamos,* a union, following which a child was born. That child was then brought up to the waiting group and presented, and the child was an ear of wheat. This derives from the death and rebirth of Dionysus, who overlaps with Osiris in association to grain symbolism (see illustration, page 64). I made that connection in order to fit it in with the sequence in diagram 3.[57]

That's the sort of thing taking place in Picture 5. Now usually this stage is not experienced consciously. Usually there's no window. It's lived, but it's not experienced. In the vast majority of cases where this cycle is initiated—endless repetitions in human history—the cycle short-circuits at Picture 5 and reverts to Picture 1, and starts over again.

You see, consciousness doesn't increase when we embrace an object of desire—that's well enough known, isn't it? That doesn't bring any consciousness, not at all. We're just satisfied and then we start over again. So ordinarily what we see here in Picture 5 is covered by a dark veil and the cycle goes no further. And I think this is pretty much what it ought to be for the first half of life.

---

[57] Above, p. 39.

# CONIVNCTIO SIVE
## *Coitus.*

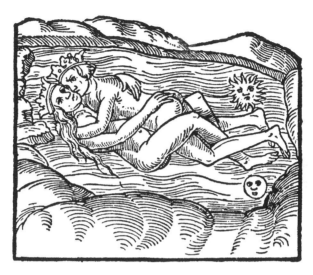

O Luna durch meyn vmbgeben/vnd suſſe mynne/
Wirſtu ſchön/ ſtarck/vnd gewaltig als ich byn·
O Sol/ du biſt vber alle liecht zu erkennen/
So bedarffſtu doch mein als der han der hennen.

# ARISLEVS IN VISIONE.
Coniunge ergo filium tuum Gabricum dilectiorem tibi in omnibus filijs tuis cum ſua ſorore
Beya

*O Luna, folded in my sweet embrace /*
*Be you as strong as I, as fair of face.*
*O Sol, brightest of all lights known to men /*
*And yet you need me, as the cock the hen.*

**Picture 5**
**Union, Manifestation of the Mystery**

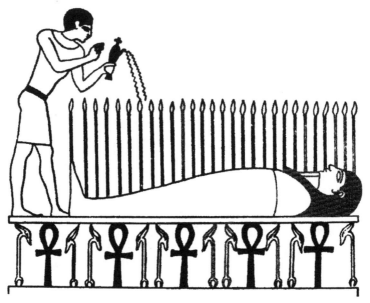

Grain growing from the corpse of Osiris
(From a bas-relief at Philae)

But there may come a time when that doesn't happen. The veil is rent, the window opens and one gets a glimpse of what's really going on psychologically. And that means a glimpse of how the opposites work. Once that's seen decisively the effect is a terrible shock. One's never the same again. So that the short-circuit of going back to Picture 1 won't work anymore; one is no longer nature's fool, so to speak. I think that comes from Shakespeare—sounds like Shakespeare doesn't it!

That's how it is in an individual. In terms of a relationship, it would indicate that the two partners have arrived at a thorough state of mutual identification. The reference here will not be primarily to concrete sexuality. Rather, it will be to what sexuality symbolizes psychologically: a state of psychological unity which I alluded to when I talked about the previous picture. This would be the culmination of that unity.

That the action takes place under water indicates its unconscious nature. This is quite a danger for one-sided solar consciousness and a parallel pic-

The "green lion" devouring the sun
*(Rosarium philosophorum,* 1550)

ture in the *Rosarium* indicates the danger. It is a picture of the sun being swallowed by a lion. The instinctual level is taking over.

As a process in the collective, Picture 5 would represent the state of affairs where the two antagonistic groups or factions have joined in a fatal embrace. The war is on, and the consequence will be determined by combat. You know that was one of the early forms of justice. Whenever there was a dispute between two factions or two individuals of any major proportion, it could be submitted to an ordeal by combat. The idea was that whoever won must have had God on his side. That psychological technique still operates in almost all collective functioning at every level, from the international to the national and right down to much smaller organizations. Ordeal by combat determines the outcome.

Commonly this would be the cut-off, the place of the short-circuit, and there'd be no going on to stage 6 but rather a reversion to stage 1. It would correspond to the state of normal ego development in which successes and accomplishments greatly outweigh failures. And that would mean a whole series of gratifications, satisfying experiences that promote ego development, promote a certain capacity for functioning by getting what one wants, going from one success and one desire to another—but it does not lead to another level of consciousness. It leads only to first half of life consciousness, not second half of life consciousness. And second half of life consciousness is what the last five pictures are about.

I should say a word or two about how this image might come up in dreams. How does one interpret the image of intercourse in dreams? Most commonly, it refers to the state of intimacy taking place between the ego and the anima or animus, depending on whether one is dealing with a masculine or a feminine ego.

Whenever I see a dream where the dreamer is in intercourse with a member of the opposite sex I immediately look for what had been going on the day before. I look for an animus attack or an anima mood—according to whether the dreamer is a woman or a man—because that's what such dreams usually refer to. They refer to an illicit affair with the anima or animus.

But such an affair is an aspect of the coniunctio, you see. It's illicit only because the ego sets up certain criteria that says it is. It's an example of merging, the ego's merging with a figure of the unconscious, and only in the short range is that subject to criticism because usually the individual's level of adaptation drops several degrees when one is in an anima or animus mood. The value of such experience is that the experience has been had; it can be the beginning of becoming aware of the nature of the anima or animus, and that then promotes the transformation of the coniunctio into a conscious experience.

If two figures other than the ego are in intercourse, that has quite a different meaning. Then it belongs more to the joining of the opposites.

*Question:* Could you say something about the number six?

Six is the second manifestation of the number three in the number series and it's represented geometrically by the overlapping of two triangles, one pointing up and the other pointing down In alchemical symbolism the downward-pointing triangle is water and the upward-pointing triangle is fire. The two together represent a union of opposites, you see.

Six is also thought of as the marriage number because the two triangles of fire and water are united in the six-pointed figure. I think that's the chief reference to the symbolism of the number six in this series of pictures.[58]

*Question:* In a dream like Picture 5, what if the two figures are of the same sex?

If they're of the same sex, it would mean that the ego and the shadow require integration. That hasn't taken place yet so the unconscious is pushing for it. It's an image of potential integration.

*Question:* In earlier pictures the moon was a crescent. In Picture 5, the moon is full. Is that significant?

I hadn't thought of that but it's an interesting observation. It would fit, wouldn't it? When you get down to the water you're in the moon realm, so naturally the moon would be full. Good point.

"Elixir of the moon"
(Codex Reginensis Latinus 1458, 17th cent.)

---

[58] For further amplification of the number 6, see "Psychology of the Transference," *Practice of Psychotherapy,* CW 16, par. 451, note 8.

**Picture 6. In the Tomb**

Things have become radically simplified! There is a mortuary slab with a united dead body on it, and that's all there is. I would remind you that this follows the picture I consider to be the revelation of the mystery. From that way of looking at it, this shows the effect of witnessing what happened in Picture 5. It literally strikes one dead.

Now there are many different ways this can be considered but the one I want to pay particular attention to, especially in terms of my earlier remarks about the opposites, is that Pictures 5 and 6 represent a consequence of seeing into the dynamism of the opposites. Once you really see how that works, you are knocked out by it, so to speak. You're suddenly ejected from the life process that has kept you going, and the shock has the effect of a kind of psychological death. Once you see behind the operation of the opposites, you're not their victim any more but at the same time you lose connection with the energy that propelled you through life.

So it's an insight that can literally kill. It's an image of what happens when one encounters a standpoint beyond the opposites and a profound wound—possibly fatal—is inflicted upon the ego. Because when the opposites are united and when one sees behind the mechanism of the opposites, then the dynamo of the psyche is broken. At least the dynamo of the ego is broken. Then there's no energy gradient between the poles to maintain a flow of life; the opposites have canceled each other out.

In terms of typical alchemical symbolism, this is an image of the mortificatio.[59] Very few alchemical operations regularly follow one another; there is as a rule no strict sequence. But there is a certain regularity to coniunctio being followed by mortificatio. If the coniunctio is not the ultimate one that totally ends the process—if it's an intermediate or lesser coniunctio[60]—then it is regularly followed by mortificatio, and that's what takes place in this picture series.

You can see a lot of examples of that if you look around. It's the theme of marriage and death: marriage being followed by death, or someone being married to Death, or a linkage of the two one way or another.[61] It is an expression of this archetypal sequence of coniunctio followed by

---

[59] See Edinger, *Anatomy,* chap. 6, "Mortificatio."

[60] Ibid., p. 211.

[61] For an example in Jung's life, see Barbara Hannah, *Jung, His Life and Work: A Biographical Memoir,* p. 346.

# PHILOSOPHORVM.
## CONCEPTIOSEV PVTRE
*factio*

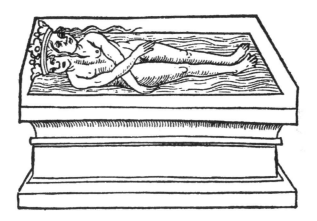

Hye ligen könig vnd köningin dot/
Die sele scheydt sich mit grosser not.

## ARISTOTELES REX ET
*Philosophus.*

Nunquam vidi aliquod animatum crescere
sine putrefactione, nisi autem fiat putris
dum inuanum erit opus alchimicum.

*Here King and Queen are lying dead /*
*In great distress the soul is sped.*

**Picture 6**
**In the Tomb**

mortificatio. Think, for instance, of Tristan and Isolde, Romeo and Juliet. One can almost say, archetypally speaking, that it is the typical fate of the lover to die. So if one is a lover, one had better disidentify from that condition somewhere along the line or risk becoming a fatality.

Another way of seeing Picture 6 is that it represents the death of the ego upon encounter with the Self. This is the sort of thing that can happen if the ego is completely identified with one side of a pair of opposites. Then, when the union takes place, the ego experiences the fate of the united opposites: the opposites die in the course of giving birth to the higher totality that transcends them, and if the ego is identified with one of those parts, it will share that death experience.

Oscar Wilde once observed that there's only one thing worse than not getting what you want, and that's getting it.[62] He lived out this sequence in his personal life, as you may know, and his defeat resulted in a considerable deepening of his psychology.

Picture 6 shows us what happens after one has united with the object that carries the projection of desire, providing consciousness arrives on the scene. As I said before, very often there's a short-circuit and the first five pictures repeat themselves. But if consciousness enters the picture, then when one gets what one wants, one discovers that isn't what one wanted. Hence the sense of disillusion and death.

*Question:* What is left after the breakdown of projection?

There's nothing left temporarily. If one's life has resided in a particular external object and then that life, that energy, leaves the object, then nothing is left of that connection. But then the missing life has to be located and it's rediscovered within. The projection has a chance to integrated.

In certain texts the alchemists state that death is the conception of the Philosophers' Stone.[63] It's a necessary beginning to the process that the development of the Philosophers' Stone represents. If Picture 10 can be called a picture of the Philosophers' Stone, then Picture 6 is its conception, the first step. And the word *conceptio* is written above Picture 6.

---

[62] The actual quote, in Wilde's play "Lady Windemere's Fan," act 3, reads: "In this world there are only two tragedies. One is not getting what one wants, and the other is getting it." *(Bartlett's Familiar Quotations,* p. 675)

[63] See, for instance, Jung's comments in "Psychology of the Transference," *Practice of Psychotherapy,* CW 16, par. 473.

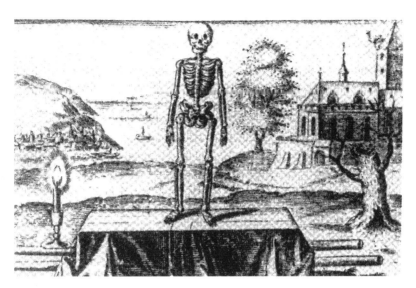

Skeleton as image of mortificatio
(From A.E. Waite, trans., *The Hermetic Museum*)

Here's what Jung says about the psychology of this event:

> The integration of contents that were always unconscious and projected involves a serious lesion of the ego. Alchemy expresses this through the symbols of death, mutilation, or poisoning.[64]

And that is what is represented in Picture 6.

So the encounter of the smaller entity, the ego, with the Self evokes a damage that borders on the fatal. I think it's very similar to what happens when a primitive society encounters a more highly developed society.

Let's consider a little further the aspects of mortificatio symbolism. I'll give you a couple of alchemical texts that refer to this, just for the flavor.

> Oh happy gate of blackness, cries the sage, which art the passage to this so glorious change. Study, therefore, whosoever appliest himself to this Art, only to know this secret, for to know this is to know all, but to be ignorant of this is to be ignorant of all. For putrefaction precedes the generation of every new form into existence.[65]

---

[64] Ibid., par. 472.

[65] Scholia to "The Golden Treatise of Hermes," quoted in M.A. Atwood, *Hermetic Philosophy and Alchemy,* pp. 126f.

Putrefaction is one aspect of mortificatio. It's just one step further—you die and then you rot. Here's what one alchemical text says about it:

> Putrefaction is of so great efficacy that it blots out the old nature and trans-
> mutes everything into another new nature, and bears another new fruit. All
> living things die in it, all dead things decay, and then all these dead things
> regain life. Putrefaction takes away the acridity from all corrosive spirits of
> salt, renders them soft and sweet.[66]

That's paradoxical thinking; the idea is that putrefaction which stinks and is foul brings about sweet and soft consequences.

Most frequently in the texts it is the king, or Sol, that undergoes the mortificatio. In the *Rosarium* sequence it is Sol and Luna simultaneously. For a man, Sol would represent the archetypal principle of ego functioning, and Luna would represent the same for a woman. It's that kind of egocentricity that must be mortified at a certain stage. Jung says, for instance:

> Egocentricity is a necessary attribute of consciousness and is also its specific
> sin. [67]

And mortificatio is the eventual punishment of that sin.

How would this image show up in the various modes we've spoken of? In an individual, it would picture the situation where the ego has been united with the desired object and then experiences disillusionment. It would follow not just any old event but rather some crucial experience coming at a time when a new level of consciousness was ready to emerge. Then, after getting what one thought one wanted, to discover that one has been seeking the wrong thing all along has the effect of a revelation.

Or it can be an image of just the opposite—of failing to get what one wanted, of being frustrated. And, because the time is right, one does not just drop the issue and go hunting in greener pastures but chooses, or is obliged, to endure to the bitter full the frustration of not getting what one thought one wanted. In that process of defeat and mortificatio, one then makes the transition to another level of awareness.

You see, either way it's an experience of defeat. If you get what you wanted and discover you didn't want it after all, that's every bit as much a defeat as not getting it—in some respects, it's worse because you did it

---

[66] Paracelsus, *The Hermetic and Alchemical Writings of Paracelsus,* 1: 153.

[67] *Mysterium Coniunctionis,* CW 14, par. 364.

yourself.

In terms of a relationship, we could think of it as representing two people who have merged psychologically in ways I've talked about earlier, who in the course of that merging lose their separate identities and then discover that fact. If you don't realize what's happened, you don't get past Picture 5; but if you do discover the fact that in your dependent merging into a state of *participation mystique* with your partner you've lost your identity, then that's experienced as a death—it's a death that's already happened but it doesn't register until one becomes aware of it, you see. It only becomes a disaster when it's discovered. But the discovery of it then allows the process to continue and the next stages, represented in Pictures 7 to 10, to occur.

If we consider Picture 6 as representing a process in a collective, then we might say that the war between the two factions is over. It took place in Picture 5 and it's finished. The issue is decided; presumably both are exhausted, one in victory and one in defeat. And the same issues will apply if the process isn't to be short-circuited. You may have noticed in the history of nations that often the nation defeated in war later rises to a higher level of collective development than the victorious one. At any rate, the experience of defeat must also take place in the collectivity in order for this image to emerge. Naturally it will take place more readily with the faction that's been defeated, but it can also take place in the victorious nation, for instance if it's been a Pyrrhic victory, or the awareness dawns that the war wasn't worth fighting after all.

However, from this point on, I don't feel able to pursue this sequence of pictures further in terms of the collective process. Maybe somebody else can do it, but from here on I'm only able to interpret it as a process within an individual. I believe collective or dual interpretations peter out with Picture 6 and if anyone disagrees with me, I'll be happy to listen.[68]

Now, Picture 6 is not at all an uncommon image in dreams—the image of the death of some figure—and that would represent a process of transformation. I always understand death in dreams as being part of the larger theme of death and rebirth, and if the rebirth isn't evident in one dream, it will almost always show up, sooner or later, in a future one.

But of course the image has the greatest impact when it's the dreamer

---

[68] This is not to say that an individual who consciously carries the opposites within does not have an inductive effect on a relationship and on the collective. See above, pp. 25-26, and Edinger, *The Mysterium Lectures,* pp. 310ff.

who has the experience of dying. That's not so common but it's not rare either, and in my experience it never means literal death. Rather, it means a very sizable attitudinal change. Sizable enough for the unconscious to express it in terms of death—the old ego and its governing principles are being modified or altered to such an extent that it's felt to be an actual death.

*Question:* Could you comment on the hermaphroditic quality of the inert being in Picture 6?

I can reiterate something Jung says on the subject, which is that in actual clinical material, in his experience—and the same thing applies to my own experience—the image of the hermaphrodite is not an image of the final product. It is rather an image of the original composite mixture, the *prima materia,* that needs to undergo differentiation.[69]

## Picture 7. Separation of Soul and Body

Now things become a little more complex again. More elements enter the picture. We have the same slab tomb with the united body lying on it, but in addition a tiny little figure is ascending from the body into a cloud that has appeared above the tomb.

This is a representation of the age-old image of the soul separating from the body at the moment of death. You find this pictured very graphically in some of the old texts—in Homer for instance. As the individual died, on-lookers thought they actually saw a little smoke-like wraith leave the mouth of the dying body and ascend. And that was understood as the soul departing the body at the moment of death. It was very much associated with the breath, of course, because breathing in and out is evidence that the soul still occupies the body; when the breathing stops, then the soul has left the body. I've heard of several similar experiences of people witnessing a death and having a vivid sense of the soul leaving the body, very often associated with wind-like qualities.

Psychologically it corresponds, in smaller ways anyway, to what happens when any sizable identification or projection breaks down. A piece of

---

[69] See Jung's comments on Picture 9 in "Psychology of the Transference," *Practice of Psychotherapy,* CW 16, par. 494.

# ROSARIVM
## ANIMÆ EXTRACTIO VEL
*imprægnatio*

**ʒye teylen ſich die vier element/**
**Aus dem leyb ſcheydt ſich die ſele behendt.**

Dε

*Here is the division of the four elements /*
*As from the lifeless corpse the soul ascends.*

**Picture 7**
**Separation of Soul and Body**

the psyche separates from the concrete, corporeal container. You know, as long as we have pieces of our psyche deposited, like bank deposits actually, in various objects or activities or people in our outside environment—as long as that's the case, then there's a free-flow of life, a kind of breathing between ourselves and those parts of our exteriorized psyche. Life goes on; one is interested and alive and things flow.

Now if any of those containers of one's psyche dies, one goes through a grief reaction because a piece of one's self dies at the same time. A kind of separation is required. One has to take back that piece of one's own psyche from the person who has died, otherwise it will pull us into the grave too.

The same thing can happen when a person or object dies for us psychologically—it doesn't have to be a literal death. There's a psychological death when the projection that has been carried for us drops off. A piece of on-going life we were used to has disappeared, and we are in effect dead until that missing piece of our psyche is recovered. That's the sort of process Picture 7 represents.

I came across quite a striking dream example of this image. Some years ago I made a move from New York to California, which involved a certain upset for some of the patients I was working with, as you can imagine. One particular patient, on the day I was going to inform him about my move two months hence, the very day I was going to tell him, brought me this dream:

> I was watching the following scene: I saw my own corpse laid out on a stretcher and, as though in demonstration, the flesh fell off the bones of my leg. It was like seeing a chicken where the flesh fell away easily from the bone. I said to myself, "That is my corpse!" Then a voice said, "The soul needs an hour to leave the body. It is important that you help keep the body together for an hour until the soul can make a proper exit."
>
> This remark was presumably directed to an attendant, and then, again as though in demonstration, something cloud-like or vaporous was sucked up out of my mouth.

There's the ancient image repeated in a modern dream.

It was immediately evident to me that this dream referred to what I hadn't yet told my patient. And of course it told me that things must not be done too hastily because "the soul needs an hour to leave the body." The dreamer's association to an hour was an analytic hour. I don't think it was just for this reason alone, but I did arrange things so that for a year or more I commuted between New York and California and terminated the analysis very gradually. It worked out all right, but isn't it astonishing that the unconscious could present a dream of this depth and import? To me it was a measure of the fact that the analytic process was absolutely crucial to this man, a matter of life and death.

Now, there are four pictures in the *Rosarium* series—Pictures 6, 7, 8 and 9, showing the death, the separation and ascent of the soul and then the return of the soul—that have a very definite correspondence to the three stages of the coniunctio discussed by Jung in the long last chapter of *Mysterium Coniunctionis.* I want to summarize briefly the contents of that chapter for you because I think it is essential to an adequate understanding of these pictures.[70]

With the help of a lot of alchemical texts, chiefly those from the alchemist Gerhard Dorn, Jung demonstrates that the alchemical coniunctio actually takes place in three stages. I'll just give you the bare bones of those stages.

The first stage involves the union of soul and spirit which takes place simultaneously with the separation of body and soul. It's a twofold operation in which the soul separates from the body and in the process of that separation unites with the spirit. This stage is given the Latin term *unio mentalis.* That simply means mental union, but let's use the Latin to indicate that we're talking about the technical first stage of the coniunctio: the union of soul and spirit.

In the second stage of the coniunctio, the *unio mentalis*—that entity which combines soul and spirit—reunites with the body. So now we have a union of soul, spirit and body; that's the second stage of the coniunctio.

In the third stage, that spirit-soul-body unity combines with the *unus mundus.* Or let's say it unites with the world and thereby brings about what Jung calls the *unus mundus,* which just means "one world."

Now that's not quite enough to understand what's being referred to in the last *Rosarium* pictures. We need a little bit more.

The first step involves the separation of the soul from the body, and then the other half of that step—the union of soul and spirit— happens automatically. Jung says about this:

> In order to bring about their subsequent reunion, the mind . . . must be separated from the body—which is equivalent to "voluntary death"—for only separated things can unite. . . . [This involves a] discrimination and dissolu-

---

[70] For a fuller discussion, see Edinger, *Mysterium Lectures,* lectures 23-27.

tion of the "composite," the composite state being one in which the affectivity of the body has a disturbing influence on the rationality of the mind. The aim of this separation was to free the mind from the influence of the "bodily appetites and the heart's affections," and to establish a spiritual position which is supraordinate to the turbulent sphere of the body. This leads at first to a dissociation of the personality and a violation of the merely natural man.

This preliminary step, in itself a clear blend of Stoic philosophy and Christian psychology, is indispensable for the differentiation of consciousness. Modern psychotherapy makes use of the same procedure when it objectifies the affects and instincts and confronts consciousness with them.[71]

What that means is that in the vital first stage of the coniunctio, the dissociation between the spiritual pole of the psyche and the bodily pole must be complete. You could say that that's what the last two thousand years or more of cultural history has been working on—the first stage of the coniunctio. It started with the Stoic philosophers and Christianity picked it up. As Nietzsche very cleverly put it, "Christianity is Platonism for the people."[72] But it has all been part of the effort to bring about a thorough first stage of the coniunctio.

When that's been brought about, one is immune from being possessed by the "bodily affections"—that's what it amounts to. Of course one is split, and the images that go to picture this first stage are such things as decapitation—not very agreeable. But when that stage has been fully achieved, the affects have been contained.

Then the second stage takes on importance—reuniting the *unio mentalis* with the body. That means everything that one had to dissociate from at the previous stage has to be reincorporated at a new level of consciousness. You have to do everything you did before, let the same energies back in, but they are altogether different because they're accompanied by consciousness. In effect those energies and their sources have undergone a death and rebirth. They've been regenerated. First they've been killed and then they've been reborn.

The third stage of the coniunctio, called the union with the *unus mundus*, I'll say a little more about when we come to Picture 10, but I think it's beyond our power to describe very specifically because it signifies a union with the totality that probably belongs only, in a really full sense, with the experience of death.

---

[71] *Mysterium Coniunctionis,* CW 14, pars. 671f.

[72] *Beyond Good and Evil,* p. 3.

Speaking of Plato, I want to read you a particularly pertinent remark about the nature of death. Here's how the Greek philosophers thought of death and it's absolutely relevant to the nature of the first stage of the coniunctio. This is Socrates speaking while he's waiting in prison to die after drinking hemlock:

> Is not what we call death a freeing and separation of soul from body? . . . And the desire to free the soul is found chiefly, or rather only, in the true philosopher. In fact the philosopher's occupation consists precisely in the freeing and separation of soul from body. . . . If a man has trained himself throughout his life to live in a state as close as possible to death, would it not be ridiculous for him to be distressed when death comes to him?

And here's the punch line:

> True philosophers make dying their profession, and . . . to them of all men death is least alarming. . . . If they are thoroughly dissatisfied with the body, and long to have their souls independent of it [that states in a nutshell the first stage of the coniunctio], when this happens would it not be entirely unreasonable to be frightened and distressed? Would they not naturally be glad to set out for the place where there is a prospect of attaining the object of their lifelong desire—which is wisdom—and of escaping from an unwelcome association?[73]

This is a marvelous example of the whole human effort to set up a spiritual counterpole against nature, body and instinct; it belongs to our finest cultural tradition and is relevant to the first stage of the coniunctio. And psychologically what it refers to is the withdrawal of projections. I told you what happens when a projection drops off—death follows.

Now two new things show up in Picture 7: the little homunculus signifying the soul, and the cloud.

Jung remarks about this in "The Psychology of the Transference":

> The psychological interpretation of this process leads into regions of inner experience which defy our powers of scientific description, however unprejudiced or even ruthless we may be. At this point, unpalatable as it is to the scientific temperament, the idea of mystery forces itself upon the mind of the inquirer, not as a cloak for ignorance but as an admission of his inability to translate what he knows into the everyday speech of the intellect. I must therefore content myself with a bare mention of the archetype which is inwardly experienced at this stage, namely the birth of the "divine child" or—in the language of the mystics—the inner man.[74]

---

[73] Plato, *Phaedo*, 67c-68b, in *The Collected Dialogues*.

[74] *Practice of Psychotherapy*, CW 16, par. 482.

So Jung takes the emergence of this little homunculus figure to represent the birth of the divine child, the inner man. And it's born out of the death of the body, meaning death of the concrete level of human existence, the level of *participation mystique* I've already alluded to.

The other new entity appearing in Picture 7 is the cloud and it's very important. The cloud is one of the age-old symbolic images of transpersonal reality; it's how the numinosum manifests. Let me give you a few examples just to remind you. For instance, in antiquity, Zeus was represented as seated on a cloud. For the Israelites, during their wanderings in the wilderness, Yahweh went before them, by day in a pillar of cloud to lead the way, and by night, in a pillar of fire. Yahweh came to Moses in a cloud on Mount Sinai. We read:

> The cloud covered the mountain, and the glory of Yahweh settled on the mountain of Sinai; for six days the cloud covered it, and on the seventh day Yahweh called to Moses from inside the cloud.[75]

When Solomon's temple was completed, it was meant quite literally to house Yahweh. The Ark of the Covenant was placed in it and "The cloud filled the Temple of Yahweh."[76] So Yahweh came into his temple in a cloud and occupied it, because that was his dwelling place.

A cloud overshadowed Mary at the time of the Annunciation: "The Holy Ghost shall come upon thee, and the power of the Highest shall overshadow thee."[77] And at the Transfiguration of Christ: "A bright cloud covered them with shadow, and from the cloud there came a voice."[78]

In Revelation, the coming of the Apocalyptic Christ is described thus:

> And I looked, and beheld a white cloud, and upon the cloud one sat like unto the Son of man, having on his head a golden crown, and in his hand a sharp sickle.[79]

Well that will be enough to demonstrate that the cloud is an expression of the numinosum. One finds pictures in the alchemical texts of an alchemist praying, kneeling on the floor in his laboratory, and God in a cloud is instructing him how to continue with his experiments.

---

[75] Exod. 24: 16, Jerusalem Bible.

[76] 1 Kings 8: 10, Jerusalem Bible.

[77] Luke 1: 35, Authorized Version.

[78] Matt. 17: 5, Jerusalem Bible.

[79] Rev. 14: 14, Authorized Version.

These are all relevant associations to the meaning of the cloud which now appears here for the first time, following the experience of death. That is characteristic, for the death of the ego is a necessary prelude to the theophany. You see, it's the same as the sequence of the death and rebirth of the Year Spirit.[80]

Alchemist praying to God in a cloud
(Barchusen, *Elementa chemiae,* 1718)

---

[80] See above, pp. 38-39.

**Picture 8. Gideon's Dew Drips from the Cloud**

Now the homunculus has disappeared into the cloud, which is still present, and the dead united body remains on the slab. The new feature is that dew starts dripping from the cloud. In the previous picture a movement from below upward was taking place, from the body to the cloud. Now, with the descent of the dew, a movement is initiated in the reverse direction—from above downward. This is a very important image with deep psychological implications.

The text that accompanies Picture 8 calls this Gideon's dew, and we must talk a bit about that. Every now and then it happens that a dream says something absolutely explicit. I'm referring to dreams that mention very specific mythological motifs. Those are especially important because they are telling the dreamer unambiguously, "Look, this is the myth you're living out."

Well, these alchemical texts are the same as dream documents and here we have one that's doing the same thing; it doesn't just say dew dripped from the cloud, it says Gideon's dew dripped from the cloud. So that will be telling the alchemist who's performing this experiment, "You're living out the myth of Gideon." Let's go to that myth and see what that would be.

We find it in the sixth chapter of Judges. At this time in history, Israel was occupied by a foreign power, by Midianites. And the Midianites had imposed their religion and were sacrificing to their gods ostentatiously to demonstrate their occupying status. In that situation Yahweh visited a young man called Gideon. Here's what he says:

> Take your father's fattened calf, and pull down the altar to Baal [the altar of the alien god set up by the occupying armies] belonging to your father and cut down the sacred post at the side of it. Then . . . . build a carefully constructed altar to Yahweh. . . . Then take the fattened calf and burn it as a holocaust [to Yahweh].[81]

Gideon proceeded to do what he was told. I won't go into all of this—it's a little lengthy to get to the main part.[82] Anyway that was a pretty dangerous thing to do and Gideon was almost caught for it. But that wasn't all. He got away with that but then the spirit of Yahweh came to him again

---

[81] Judges 6: 25, Jerusalem Bible.

[82] See Edinger, *The Bible and the Psyche: Individuation Symbolism in the Old Testament,* pp. 69ff.

# PHILOSOPHORVM

## ABLVTIO VEL
*Mundificatio*

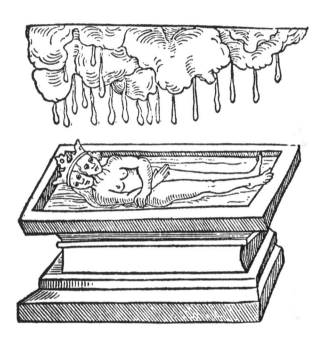

𝔥ie felt ber Tauw von 𝔥immel 𝔥erab/
𝔙nnd wafcht ben fchwarßen leyb im grab ab.·

## K iij

*Here falls the heavenly dew, to lave /*
*The soiled black body in the grave.*

**Picture 8**
**Gideon's Dew Drips from the Cloud**

and told Gideon to gather an army and start an insurrection. That's what he told him to do. And Gideon was very reluctant to do that, for it was exceedingly dangerous. So he remonstrated a bit with God, as one could do in those old times. Gideon says:

> If you really mean to deliver Israel by my hand, as you have declared, see now, I spread out a fleece on the threshing-floor; if there is dew only on the fleece and all the ground is left dry, then I shall know that you will deliver Israel by my hand, as you have declared.[83]

With this story in mind, Jung says that the picture of Gideon's dew is a "sign of divine intervention, it is the moisture that heralds the return of the soul."[84]

*Question:* Would Gideon's dew be fate?

Yes it would, that's right. It's synchronicity.

*Question:* How does rain differ from dew?

I think in dreams they can be quite similar sometimes. They're both descending but dew has a more mysterious quality. Dew comes down, but its appearance is miraculous. We wonder, where did that come from? And I think that's what particularly affects the unconscious and gives dew its miraculous quality. Rain is so obvious that it doesn't have that same nuance although it's also heavenly moisture.

*Comment:* Dew is kind of like an epiphany—it appears, like poetry.

I came across an example of this imagery concerning dew as I was doing my work on Melville's *Moby Dick*. That in many respects is a terrible book when you consider it psychologically and it gives one real concern for its author. It really disturbed me to think that a person actually went through this experience, and it was with a great sense of relief that I came to certain materials that showed up at the end of Melville's life, indicating that he had indeed integrated that devastating experience. One piece of evidence was a poem; here is the final stanza:

> Healed of my hurt, I laud the inhuman sea—
> Yea, bless the angels Four that there convene;
> For healed I am even by their pitiless breath

---

[83] Judges 6: 36-38, Jerusalem Bible; see also Edinger, *Bible and the Psyche,* p. 71.
[84] "Psychology of the Transference," *Practice of Psychotherapy,* CW 16, par. 487.

Distilled in wholesome dew named Rosemarine.[85]

Rosemarine means literally "sea dew," so you see the image of healing for Melville was one of dew. This shows what can follow the death and despair and hopelessness represented by Pictures 6 and 7.

Just to encourage you to do something I often do myself, let's take this image of dew and see what Jung might say about it in that compendium of imagery, *Mysterium Coniunctionis*. When we do that we find, among other things, the following:

> In ancient tradition Luna is the giver of moisture and ruler of the water-sign Cancer . . . . Maier says that the *umbra solis* [the shadow of the sun] cannot be destroyed unless the sun enters the sign of Cancer, but that Cancer is the "house of Luna, and Luna is the ruler of the moistures" (juice, sap, etc.). . . . Rahner, in his "Mysterium Lunae," shows the extensive use which the Church Fathers made of the allegory of the moon-dew in explaining the effects of grace . . . . Here again the patristic symbolism exerted a very strong influence on the alchemical allegories. Luna secretes the dew or sap of life. "This Luna is the sap of the water of life, which is hidden in Mercurius."
> . . . There was a principle in the moon . . . which Christianos calls the "ichor of the philosopher" . . . . The relation of the moon to the soul, much stressed in antiquity, also occurs in alchemy . . . . Usually it is said that from the moon comes the dew, but the moon is also the *aqua mirifica* [the wonderful water] that extracts the souls from the bodies or gives the bodies life and soul. Together with Mercurius, Luna sprinkles the dismembered dragon with her moisture and brings him to life again, "makes him live, walk, and run about .
> . . ." As the water of ablution, the dew falls from heaven, purifies the body, and makes it ready to receive the soul; in other words, it brings about the *albedo,* the white state of innocence, which like the moon and a bride awaits the bridegroom.[86]

So you see that's directly relevant to what we're talking about. The dew descends and purifies and revivifies the dead body. The alchemical term for this phase of the process is mundificatio—purification. You remember that the soul has been separated from the body and now, in its separated state, the body undergoes the process of purification.

I would also remind you that we should think of the body symbolically as representing a psychological entity—not the concrete literal body. It refers rather to the ego; the ego is the body of the psyche, you might say. And so what's taking place now is a purification of that dead ego by the dew, the divine dew, that's falling on it. It refers to the fact that the ego is

---

[85] "Pebbles," in *Herman Melville, Collected Poems,* p. 206.

[86] *Mysterium,* CW 14, par. 155.

to be purified from contamination with the unconscious.

I want to read you a passage where Jung refers to that:

> The process of differentiating the ego from the unconscious, then, has its equivalent in the *mundificatio* [that's what we're talking about, the purification], and, just as this is the necessary condition for the return of the soul to the body, so the body is necessary if the unconscious is not to have destructive effects on the ego-consciousness, for it is the body that gives bounds to the personality. The unconscious can be integrated only if the ego holds its ground. Consequently, the alchemist's endeavour to unite the *corpus mundum*, the purified body, with the soul is also the endeavour of the psychologist once he has succeeded in freeing the ego-consciousness from contamination with the unconscious. . . . [It comes about through the] separation of the ordinary ego-personality from all inflationary admixtures of unconscious material. This task entails the most painstaking self-examination and self-education, which can, however, be passed on to others by one who has acquired the discipline himself. . . . [It] is no light work; it needs the tenacity and patience of the alchemist, who must purify the body from all superfluities in the fiercest heat of the furnace.[87]

Another aspect of the purification of the ego is that not only must it be purified from contamination by the unconscious, it must also be separated and purified from contamination with the "eternal man." Jung refers to that in the previous paragraph:

> The rational man, in order to live in this world, has to make a distinction between "himself" and what we might call the "eternal man." Although he is a unique individual, he also stands for "man" as a species, and thus he has a share in all the movements of the collective unconscious. . . . The "eter-nal" truths become dangerously disturbing factors when they suppress the unique ego of the individual and live at his expense.[88]

What Jung is saying is that the purification process must dissolve ego-Self identity so that the ego does not remain contaminated with the eternal man. He's related to the eternal man but not identified with him. This is an exceedingly important distinction.

*Question:* There seems to be a general attempt not to extravert the process. Yet so much of it does seem to occur in an extraverted fashion. Is there any way to increase the symbolic dimension?

Well you see everything occurs on the exterior at first. The psyche is all

---

[87] "Psychology of the Transference," *Practice of Psychotherapy,* CW 16, par. 503.
[88] Ibid., par. 502

found on the outside—that's where the alchemists found it, and tribal societies even more so. It's all outside initially, because the outside and the unconscious are effectively the same thing. Whatever is unconscious is exteriorized, or at least available for exteriorization via projection. So we're constantly going through the world gathering up fragments of our own exteriorized psyche—taking back projections—and we discover where they are by our reactions, either positive or negative. Whenever we come across something that evokes a response, that means a piece of our own psyche is out there. So we go wandering around with our bags collecting these things, at least that's how I think of it.

*Question:* What exactly is the eternal man?

The Self. You see I'm defining the unknown by the unknown.

*Question:* It's not God?

Well, that's one possible term for it, too.

Alchemists at work
*(Mutus liber,* 1702)

**Picture 9. Reunion of Soul and Body**

Here the same set-up prevails: the dead united body on the slab, the cloud up above, and now the homunculus is returning. The idea would be that it's safe to go back to the body because it's been purified. And then down at the bottom we have these two birds: one standing on the ground and the other one up to its neck in the ground.

Jung suggests that the two birds represent a fledged one and an unfledged one. I would think of it as a lower version of the same event that's going on above—the one bird is looking at the buried one very much the way the descending homunculus is looking at the dead body. So I would say that the buried bird corresponds to the dead body and is on the way to being born out of its buried state, much as the dead body is about to be resurrected.

This is a picture of the second stage of the coniunctio as I spoke of it earlier. The *unio mentalis* is now reuniting with the body from which it had been separated. Some of you may know the wonderful William Blake illustration of this event (below, page 93).

Jung tells us that the *Rosarium* text accompanying Picture 9 quotes Morienus, a famous alchemist, as saying, "Despise not the ash, for it is the diadem of thy heart."[89] And Jung comments:

> This ash, the inert product of incineration, refers to the dead body, and the admonition establishes a curious connection between body and heart which at that time was regarded as the real seat of the soul. The diadem refers of course to the supremely kingly ornament. . . .
>
> The coronation picture that illustrates this text proves that the re-suscitation of the purified corpse is at the same time a glorification, since the process is likened to the crowning of the Virgin.[90]

In the *Rosarium*, the picture that accompanies our Picture 9, as a kind of parallel, is of the coronation of the Virgin Mary (see page 90). That was a very common medieval image and apparently the person who put the *Rosarium* together thought the crowning of the Virgin was analogous to this picture.

Now that parallel is not immediately obvious; it takes a little work to make the connection, just as you have to work on dream images. But when

---

[89] Ibid., par. 495.

[90] Ibid., pars. 495-496.

# PHILOSOPHORVM

## ANIMÆ IVBILATIO SEV
### Ortus seu Sublimatio.

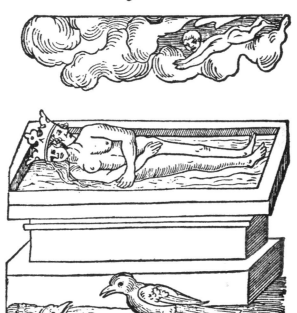

 bie schwingt sich die sele hernidder/
Vnd erquickt den gereinigten leychnam wider-

**L  iij**

*Here is the soul descending from on high /*
*To quick the corpse we strove to purify.*

**Picture 9**
**Reunion of Soul and Body**

The coronation of the Virgin Mary
*(Rosarium philosophorum,* 1550)

you do it's very revealing because as the text tells us—you may have forgotten, I keep forgetting it myself—these pictures are describing chemical processes going on in the alchemical retort. I almost forgot that! But then the text reminds me because it says this dead body lying on the slab is the ash that had been subjected to calcinatio; it had been killed and nothing is left but the dead inert stuff that's lying at the bottom of the vessel.

The end product of ash has quite interesting symbolic associations. It corresponds to what the alchemists called the "white foliated earth," which corresponds to the purified earth, the purified body. And, in spite of the ordinary associations to ash—as despair, grief and emptiness—the other set of associations are those of supreme value; they represent the whole goal of earthly existence.

For instance, recall the line just quoted: "Despise not the ashes for they are the diadem of thy heart." Another text says: "The white foliated earth is the crown of victory."[91] And another: "Sow your gold in white foliated

"Sow your gold in white foliated earth"
(Michael Maier, *Atalanta Fugiens,* 1618)

---

[91] Quoted in *Mysterium Coniunctionis,* CW 14, par. 318, note 619.

earth."[92] The ash, then, takes on the quality of the incorruptible, glorified body that has gone through the ordeal of the total process, and what's left is the supreme value.

Similar symbolism shows up in certain Biblical passages. For instance, Isaiah promises to give the mourners of Zion "a crown for ashes, the oil of joy for mourning, and a garment of praise for the spirit of grief."[93]

We have in these references a prelude to the resurrection of the glorified incorruptible body which comes in Picture 10. And the return of the separated soul to the purified body is a coronation; the body is being invested with an emblem of its supreme worth and value by the return of the soul. That event is exactly the same, symbolically, as the ascension and coronation of Mary who represents earth and materiality and body.

So Mary represents the purified white earth in the same way that the ash at the bottom of the alchemical vessel does. Egohood is redeemed and glorified.

*Question:* Where is the soul while one is waiting from Pictures 7 to 9, since the body isn't ready to receive it until Picture 9? Does the soul, while we wait, go through the transformation inside a corpse?

I don't know. I can't answer your question in those terms. You have to remember that these symbolic images cannot be approached too precisely. They are slippery; if you try to to fix them too definitively they slip right out of your hands, so you have to allow for a certain ambiguity. You have to get used to that, otherwise they just fly away.

*Question:* But in clinical experience, isn't that again a mysterious period? And if that process does occur but doesn't present itself clearly in dreams, it would be hard to have some consciousness of what's going on.

Yes, these last five pictures are all really quite mysterious and my remarks about them should be taken very tentatively.

---

[92] Michael Maier, *Atalanta Fugiens.*

[93] Isa. 61: 3, Douay Bible.

*The Reunion of the Soul and the Body*
(From Carolyn Keay, *William Blake: Selected Engravings*)

**Picture 10. Resurrection of the United Eternal Body**

The united body, combining king and queen, is now alive and erect, standing on the moon, above the earth. In the right hand is a goblet that contains three serpents, or one serpent with three heads, and each head is crowned. In the left hand, and wound around the left arm, is a fourth serpent, likewise with a crown. Out of the earth on the left side of the picture is growing a tree, which Jung tells us is the "sun and moon tree."[94] That isn't obvious from looking at it, but other alchemical illustrations show sun and moon more clearly (below). And on the other side is a single bird—the previous picture had two birds but this has just one.

Now what does all that mean? At this point I start to get vague and I must talk in symbols. It's really beyond our capacity to encompass what this image refers to; at the very best, we can just get hints about it.

The united body and the sun and moon tree
(J.D. Mylius, *Philosophia reformata,* 1622)

---

[94] "Psychology of the Transference," *Practice of Psychotherapy,* CW 16, par. 533.

# PHILOSOPHORVM.

hie ift geboren die eddele Keyferin reich/
Die meifter nennen fie ihrer dochter gleich.
Die vermeret fich/gebiert kinder ohn zal/
Sein vnd ſelich rein/vnnd ohn alles mahl.

Die

*Here is born the Empress of all honour /*
*The philosophers name her their daughter.*
*She multiplies / bears children ever again /*
*They are incorruptibly pure and without stain.*

**Picture 10**
**Resurrection of the United Eternal Body**

For one thing, it's a picture of the third stage of the coniunctio. You remember that the third stage was the union of the united body-soul-spirit entity, the purified and united body-soul-spirit with the *unus mundus*. It was a kind of cosmic union, and that's alluded to here by the fact that the figure is standing on the moon and has the sun and moon as fruit on the tree, so to speak. The idea is that the whole cosmos is a single organic pro-cess. Very occasionally one gets a glimpse of that fact—but you get the glimpse and then it fades away again and you're back in your everyday life. I think that's the implication of the sun and moon tree.

The figure is standing only on the moon, although earlier the figures were standing on both sun and moon. I think this refers to the fact that the foundation of this united eternal body is the ego. Now why do I say that? Because the opposites, sun and moon, carry with them the implication of heavenly and earthly. In comparison to each other, sun stands for heaven and moon stands for earth. That's because in antiquity the moon was thought of as the first planetary sphere and everything below that sphere— everything sublunary—belonged to the earth; psychologically speaking, it pertains to the ego. To put it another way, symbolically the ego is under the aegis of the moon. The moon is the first gateway the ego encounters on its journey up the planetary spheres.[95] And so in relation to the sun, for this figure to be standing on the moon tells me that this figure has, at its foundation, as its standpoint, ego-matter, body-matter.

I'm not going to say more about that bird. I don't know what it's doing there, except there's just one so maybe the two birds in Picture 9 got to-gether—just as the body got together. But I don't know about that.

Another thing I want to allude to are the snakes. You see we have the image of the three and the one, or the three and the four, once again. Three of them are in one container, and the other one is uncontained. But all are crowned. And if we go back to Picture 1, which is the only other picture that has a snake in it, there was no crowning there. What I think that alludes to is the transformation of the reptilian psyche.

You know the ground of our being is of that nature, it's reptilian. On unexpected occasions it can jump out and strike oneself or others just like a rattlesnake. So the fact that the snakes in Picture 10 are crowned, and also because three of them are contained in the vessel, I take to mean that the whole process of the coniunctio that led to this point has brought the reptil-

---

[95] See Edinger, *The Mysterium Lectures,* p. 101.

ian psyche into such a living connection with consciousness that it has undergone a transformation. And I think that's equivalent—to use a different symbolic terminology—to the transformation of God. It's the same psychological idea basically.[96]

*Question:* Are those wings behind the serpent?

You can't see it very clearly, but the wings belong to the united body. Both sides have wings growing out of the arms but the wing on the left doesn't reproduce very well. It's not that the serpent is winged, but the arm is winged. This is a winged being, indicating that it is a product of sublimatio. That's the idea.

*Question:* Could you say something about sublimatio?

Sublimation is an upward movement from below. It refers to a chemical event in which, if certain substances are heated—mercury is an outstanding example of this—they vaporize and then condense or crystallize on the cooler portions of the vessel; that is called sublimation or sublimatio.[97]

The *Rosarium* also includes another picture, a parallel to Picture 10. It's a representation of Christ rising out of his tomb as a symbol of the *filius philosophorum* (see next page). This is an example of the Christ-lapis parallel that Jung discusses at length in *Psychology and Alchemy*.[98]

I understand this image, and Picture 10, to refer to the creation of a psychic substance that has a nontemporal or eternal dimension to it, a kind of incorruptibility. It is an expression of the product of an ego that has experienced the process of individuation. This necessarily has a certain hypothetical quality about it because it can't be demonstrated in any decisive, irrefutable way, but a great many images point to this idea and I think it does no harm to state it explicitly. One can then entertain it and see how it feels, see how the unconscious responds to having it stated so explicitly.

The idea is that if one lives life in the fashion represented by this series of ten pictures, if one lives an alchemical life, one creates a product. And that product has a life and a quality and an existence beyond temporal existence. We have a lot of indications that the psyche transcends space and time—we don't know that the personal psyche transcends space and time

---

[96] See Edinger, *The Creation of Consciousness,* chap. 4.

[97] See Edinger, *Anatomy,* chap. 5, "Sublimatio."

[98] CW 12, chap. 5.

The Risen Christ as symbol of the *filius philosophorum*
*(Rosarium philosophorum,* 1550)

but we do know that the psyche does. And there are reasons to believe that the products of the ego's efforts may transcend space and time. To the extent that they achieve an impersonal quality, it isn't exactly the personal psyche that does that transcending, but it is as a result of the ego's opus.

To conclude I'd like to read you the poem that accompanies Picture 10 in which this united eternal body describes herself. I'll read the whole thing first to give you the overall flavor, and then I'll go back over some of the lines and make some remarks that may clarify them. So what isn't understandable on the first reading, I hope will become so.

Here's the poem:

Here is born the Empress of all honour /
The philosophers name her their daughter.
She multiplies / bears children ever again /
They are incorruptibly pure and without stain.
The Queen hates death and poverty
She surpasses gold silver and jewellery /
All medicaments great and small.
Nothing upon earth is her equal /
Wherefore we say thanks to God in heaven.

Then she speaks:

O force constrains me naked woman that I am /
For unblest was my body when I first began.
And never did I become a mother /
Until the time when I was born another.
Then the power of roots and herbs did I possess /
And I triumphed over all sickness.
Then it was that I first knew my son /
And we two came together as one.
There I was made pregnant by him and gave birth
Upon a barren stretch of earth.
I became a mother yet remained a maid /
And in my nature was establishèd.
Therefore my son was also my father /
As God ordained in accordance with nature.
I bore the mother who gave me birth /
Through me she was born again upon earth.
To view as one what nature hath wed /
Is in our mountain most masterfully hid.
Four come together in one /
In this our magisterial Stone.
And six when seen as a trinity /
Is brought to essential unity.
To him who thinks on these things aright /
God giveth the power to put to flight
All such sicknesses as pertain
To metals and the bodies of men.
None can do that without God's help /
And then only if he see through himself.
Out of my earth a fountain flows /
And into two streams it branching goes.

> One of them runs to the Orient /
> The other towards the Occident.
> Two eagles fly up with feathers aflame /
> Naked they fall to earth again.
> Yet in full feather they rise up soon /
> That fountain is Lord of sun and moon.
> O Lord Jesu Christ who bestow'st
> The gift through the grace of thy Holy Ghost:
> He unto whom it is given truly /
> Understands the masters' sayings entirely.
> That his thoughts on the future life may dwell /
> Body and soul are joined so well.
> And to raise them up to their father's kingdom /
> Such is the way of art among men.[99]

This is a description of the Philosophers' Stone. It is also a description of the eternal conscious body that I tried to outline a moment ago. Now, let's look at a few of the specific statements and see how they would apply psychologically.

> The philosophers name her their daughter.

More often the philosophers, the alchemists, name their Stone (which is the united eternal body shown in Picture 10) their son but the meaning is the same. Daughter seems more relevant here, doesn't it, since it's standing on the moon.

> She multiplies / bears children ever again /

This is a reference to the multiplicatio, which is an amazing and important aspect of the Philosophers' Stone.[100] The idea is that once the Philosophers' Stone has been made it has the power to replicate itself. If you take a bit of Philosophers' Stone as a very fine powder and throw it on to base matter, it turns whatever it touches into more Philosophers' Stone. It multiplies itself. I think this is very significant symbolism psychologically. It says to me that every time an individual has succeeded to some extent in achieving a relation to the Self, that achievement has a tendency to be contagious, to affect others—to multiply. Of course it has to meet matter that's open to receive it in order for multiplicatio to take effect, but I see it

---

[99] "Psychology of the Transference," *Practice of Psychotherapy*, CW 16, par. 528.
[100] See Edinger, *Anatomy*, pp. 227-228.

happening all the time.

> They are incorruptibly pure and without stain.

I would understand this to mean that the eternal body is not contaminated with unconsciousness. The symbolism of purity, in psychological terms, means that we are conscious of our dirt, not that we don't have dirt but it's purified dirt because we're conscious of it. And that makes all the difference.

> She surpasses . . . All medicaments great and small.

That would refer to the healing capacity, the ability to make whole.

> And I triumphed over all sickness.

This would correspond to one of the synonyms for the Philosophers' Stone which is "panacea"—the cure of everything. Now, what does that mean psychologically? It certainly does not mean that contact with the Self makes one immune to sickness. I think it means, rather, that all vicissitudes of life, including illness, become meaningful when experienced in relation to the Self and therefore promote the experience of wholeness. They don't bring about dissociation. So it isn't so much that one is immune to sickness or death, which is certainly not the case, but rather that such experiences are part of the meaningful whole and one is healed in the midst of sickness, so to speak.

> Then it was that I first knew my son /
> And we two came together as one.
> There I was made pregnant by him and gave birth
> . . . . . . . . . . . . . . . . . . . . .
> Therefore my son was also my father.

This is a remarkable section, which I understand psychologically to refer to the relation between the ego and the Self. The Self gives birth to the ego initially—the unconscious Self gives birth to the ego—which is then the major seat of consciousness for a period of time. Then, if the ego earnestly pursues a relation to the unconscious and there develops the kind of sequence that the *Rosarium* pictures represent, the effect is that the ego, the son of the unconscious, becomes the parent of the regenerate or reborn Self. This is psychological incest, that tabooed subject. Freud discovered the incest archetype but understood it only personalistically. Jung discovered its transpersonal level.[101] The Philosophers' Stone is a product of incest—a crime on the concrete level and a sacred mystery on the inner psychological level.

For the Philosophers' Stone to say "My son was also my father" is a quaint way of putting it but it makes sense when you think of it that way. It emphasizes the crucial importance of the ego for the success of the opus, and this is one of the special features of the whole alchemical enterprise that is unique to the Western psyche. Even when the alchemists maintain that the opus will only succeed *Deo concedente,* God willing, and with an appropriate religious attitude, nevertheless there's no question that the opus will ever take place by itself; it has to have an alchemist, an ego. And indeed some of these alchemists were very profound examples of life-long service and commitment to the process. Therefore the product of the process was entitled to be called the son or daughter of the alchemist.

> None can do that without God's help /
> And then only if he can see through himself.

These two lines are quite striking and overtly psychological. For this particular author anyway, it was perfectly clear that self-knowledge was an essential ingredient of the opus.

> Two eagles fly up with feathers aflame /
> Naked they fall to earth again.

The two eagles flying up "with feathers aflame," falling to earth and then rising again—phoenix-like—is an image of the combination of sublimatio and coagulatio, which is what takes place in this sequence of pictures. The descending dove in Pictures 2, 3 and 4 is an image of coagulatio[102]—of a spirit entity that descends into earthly existence and incarnates. And then the ascending homunculus, in Picture 7, is an image of the upward, sublimatio movement which is followed by another descent in Pictures 8 and 9. So all together it's a representation of the circulatio, a repeated circuit of all aspects of one's being which gradually unites the opposites.[103]

The final words in this profound poem are these:

> He unto whom it is given truly /

---

[101] See espec. *Symbols of Transformation,* CW 5 (index entries under "incest").

[102] See Edinger, *Anatomy,* chap. 4.

[103] Ibid., pp. 142ff.

Understands the masters' sayings entirely.
That his thoughts on the future life may dwell /
Body and soul are joined so well.
And to raise them up to their father's kingdom /
Such is the way of art among men.

That I understand, to use the ecclesiastical imagery the alchemists were familiar with, as an expression of the creation of the eternal body.

"Thoughts on the future life" refers to the eternal, nontemporal dimension, and "to raise up [the fruits of one's efforts] to the father's kingdom" likewise indicates a translation of the consequence of the life of the ego into the archetypal dimension.

As I see it, the fruits of the life of a person who has lived through this process can be deposited in a kind of archetypal treasury and provide an increment to it. The father's kingdom, so to speak, is thereby augmented by the alchemical efforts—the individuation process—of the individual ego.

And that task, I believe, belongs to each one of us.

Alchemists at work
*(Mutus liber,* 1702)

# Bibliography

Atwood, M.A. *Hermetic Philosophy and Alchemy*. 1850. Reprint. New York: The Julian Press, 1960.

*Bartlett's Familiar Quotations*. New York: Little, Brown, 1980.

*The Belles Heures of Jean, Duke of Berry*. New York: Georges Braziller, 1974.

Edinger, Edward F. *Anatomy of the Psyche: Alchemical Symbolism in Psychotherapy*. La Salle, IL: Open Court, 1985.

_____. *The Bible and the Psyche: Individuation Symbolism in the Old Testament*. Toronto: Inner City Books, 1986.

_____. *The Christian Archetype: A Jungian Commentary on the Life of Christ*. Toronto: Inner City Books, 1987.

_____. *The Creation of Consciousness: Jung's Myth for Modern Man*. Toronto: Inner City Books, 1984.

_____. *Encounter with the Self: A Jungian Commentary on William Blake's* Illustrations of the Book of Job. Toronto: Inner City Books, 1986.

_____. *Goethe's Faust: Notes for a Jungian Commentary*. Toronto: Inner City Books, 1990.

_____. *Melville's Moby Dick: A Jungian Commentary (An American Nekyia)*. New York: New Directions, 1978.

_____. *The Mysterium Lectures: A Journey Through C.G. Jung's Mysterium Coniunctionis*. Toronto: Inner City Books, 1995.

_____. *Transformation of the God Image: An Elucidation of Jung's* Answer to Job. Toronto: Inner City Books, 1992.

Emerson, Ralph Waldo. *Selected Writings of Ralph Waldo Emerson*. Ed. Brooks Atkinson. New York: Modern Library, 1940.

Hannah, Barbara. *Jung, His Life and Work: A Biographical Memoir*. New York: G.P. Putnam's Sons, 1976.

Jung, C.G. *C.G. Jung Speaking: Interviews and Encounters* (Bollingen Series XCVII). Ed. Wm. McGuire, R.F.C. Hull. Princeton: Princeton University Press, 1977.

_____. *The Collected Works of C.G. Jung* (Bollingen Series XX). 20 vols. Trans. R.F.C. Hull. Ed. H. Read, M. Fordham, G. Adler, Wm. McGuire. Princeton: Princeton University Press, 1953-1979.

_____. *Letters* (Bollingen Series XCV). 2 vols. Trans. R.F.C. Hull. Ed. G. Adler,

A. Jaffé. Princeton: Princeton University Press, 1973.

_____. *Man and His Symbols.* London: Aldus Books, 1964.

_____. *Memories, Dreams, Reflections.* Ed. Aniela Jaffé. New York: Random House, 1963.

_____. *The Visions Seminars.* 2 vols. Zürich: Spring Publications, 1976.

Keay, Caroline. *William Blake: Selected Engravings.* New York: St. Martin's Press, 1975.

Klossowski de Rola, Stanislas. *Alchemy: The Secret Art.* London: Thames and Hudson, 1973

*The Lives of the Alchemistical Philosophers.* London: John M. Watkins, 1955.

Maier, Michael. *Atalanta Fugiens,* 1618. Pamphlet reprint. Berkeley, n.d.

Melville, Herman. *Herman Melville, Collected Poems.* Ed. Howard P. Vincent. Chicago: Packard and Co., Hendricks House, 1947.

Michelangelo. *The Sonnets of Michelangelo.* Trans. Elizabeth Jennings. Garden City, NY: Doubleday, 1970.

*Morris' Human Anatomy.* Ed. J. Parsons Schaeffer. 10th ed. Philadelphia: The Blakiston Co., 1943.

Murray, Gilbert. "Excursus on the Ritual Forms Preserved in Greek Tragedy." In *Epilelogomena to the Study of Greek Religion and Themis.* Ed. Jane Ellen Harrison. New Hyde Park, NY: University Books, 1962.

Neumann, Erich, *The Origins and History of Consciousness* (Bollingen Series XLII). Trans. R.F.C. Hull. Princeton: Princeton University Press, 1970.

Nietzsche, Friedrich. *Beyond Good and Evil.* Trans. Walter Kaufmann. New York: Random House, 1966.

Paracelsus. *The Hermetic and Alchemical Writings of Paracelsus.* Trans. and ed. A.E. Waite. New Hyde Park, NY: University Books, 1967.

Perera, Sylvia Brinton. *The Scapegoat Complex: Toward a Mythology of Shadow and Guilt.* Toronto: Inner City Books, 1986.

Plato. *Phaedo.* In *The Collected Dialogues.* Ed. Edith Hamilton and Huntington Cairns: New York: Pantheon, 1961.

Waite, A.E., trans. *The Hermetic Museum.* York Beach, ME: Samuel Weiser, Inc., 1991.

# Index

Page numbers in *italics* refer to illustrations

Mount Sinai, 80
multiplicatio, 100-101
Murray, Gilbert, 38
*Mutus liber, 8, 31, 87, 103*
Mylius, J.D., *59, 94*
*Mysterium Coniunctionis:* 7-30, 33,
54, 72, 77, 85, 91
as anatomy of the psyche, 10
as bread, 9-10
*Mysterium Lectures, The,* 18, 43, 77,
96

"naked truth," 52
Neumann, Erich, 13, 56, 58
Nietzsche, Friedrich, 78
numbers, 12, 42-43
numinosum/numinosity, 12, 80-81
Nut, sky goddess, 12, *13*

opposites: 7, 11-19, 21-22, 24-25,
28-30, 38, 50, 52, 56, 58, 64, 68,
70-74, 102
emergence of, *34,* 36, *37,* 38, 44,
*45,* 46-50
separation of, 12, *13,* 44, 56
union of, *see* coniunctio
ordeal by combat, 65
*Origins and History of
Consciousness, The,* 13, 56
Osiris, 18, 62, *64*

Paracelsus, 72
paradox, 19-20, 46, 72
*participation mystique,* 56, 58, 73, 80
*Pathos,* 38, *39*
Perera, Sylvia Brinton, 14
persona, 52-53
*pharmakon athanasias,* 18
Philosophers' Stone, 10, 18-19, 29,
42, 70-71, 100-102
*Philosophia reformata, 59, 94*
philosophical tree, *31*
"Philosophical Tree, The," 7
Plato/Platonism, 78-79
possession, 21, 29, 78

*prima materia,* 36, 40, 54, 74
projection, 7-8, 16-17, 26-27, 56, 70-
71, 74, 76, 79, 87
psychic energy, *see* libido
*Psychology and Alchemy,* 97
"Psychology of the Transference,
The," 27, 33, 49, 52, 67, 70, 74,
79-80, 84, 86, 94
purification, 85-86, 88, 91
putrifaction, 71-72
Pythagoreans, 12, 43

quaternity, 42
queen, 44, *45,* 54, *55,* 94, *95*
quintessence, 40, 44

rain, 84
redemption, of society, 25-26
relationship, 40, 48-49, 52-53, 58,
60, 64, 73
repression, 27-28
resurrection, *36-37,* 38, 92, 94, *95, 98*
reunion of soul and body, *36-37,* 38,
88,
*89,* 91-92, *93*
*Reunion of the Soul and the Body, 93*
"Ripley Scrowle," *53*
ritual, 15-16
Romeo and Juliet, 70
*Rosarium* cycle, 36, *37,* 38
*Rosarium philosophorum:* 26, 33-
103
pictures in, 26, 33, *34-36, 41,
45, 51, 55, 63, 65, 69, 75, 83,
89, 90, 95, 98*
ways of looking at, 39-40
rose, *53*
rosemarine, 85

*Scapegoat Complex, The,* 14
"Secret Book of Artephius, The," 54
Self: 16-17, 19-20, 47, 60, 87, 100
and ego, 22-23, 29, 70-71, 86-87,
101-102
separatio, 44

# Studies in Jungian Psychology
## by Jungian Analysts        Quality Paperbacks

*Prices and payment in $US (except in Canada, $Cdn)*

*The Call of Destiny: An Introduction to Carl Jung's Major Works*
  J. Gary Sparks ISBN 9781738738502. 10 Illustrations. Index. 192pp. $28

*Sacred Chaos: God's Shadow and the Dark Self*
  Francoise O'Kane ISBN 9780919123656. Index. 144pp. $25

*The Cassandra Complex: Living with Disbelief*
  Laurie L. Schapira ISBN 9780919123359. Index. 160pp. $25

*Conscious Femininity: Interviews with Marion Woodman*
  Marion Woodman ISBN 9780919123595. Index. 160pp. $25

*The Love Drama of C. G. Jung*
  Maria Helena Mandacarú Guerra ISBN 9781894574426. Index. 128pp. $25

*The Problem of the Puer Aeternus*
  Marie-Louise von Franz ISBN 9780919123885. Index. 288pp. $40

*Personality Types: Jung's Model of Typology*
  Daryl Sharp ISBN 9780919123304. Index. 128pp. $25

*Live your Nonsense: Halfway to Dawn with Eros*
  Daryl Sharp ISBN 9781894574310. Index. 128pp. $25

*Encounter with the Self: William Blake's Illustrations of the Book of Job*
  Edward F. Edinger ISBN 9780919123212. 22 illustrations. Index. 80pp. $25

**INNER CITY BOOKS**
21 Milroy Crescent.
Toronto ON M1C 4B6 Canada
416-927-0355  www.innercitybooks.net

# Audiobooks

Audiobook editions of the titles below are sold directly from Amazon and other places where you buy your audiobooks. Not all titles are available from all places. Audiobooks are convenient, great for long trips, and can be a boon to those with vision impairment. Current audiobooks include these titles with many more to come:

*Swamplands of the Soul*
*The Eden Project*
*Under Saturn's Shadow*
  James Hollis

*Addiction to Perfection*
  Marion Woodman

*The Call of Destiny*
  J. Gary Sparks

*Transformation of the God-Image*
  Edward F. Edinger

~

# eBooks

eBooks are digital versions of printed books that can be purchased, downloaded, then viewed on a computer and some eReader devices. Many of our titles are available as eBooks, on our website in ePUB and/or PDF format, or from Amazon as Kindle Books.

Browse eBooks on our website below.

**INNER CITY BOOKS**
**21 Milroy Crescent.**
**Toronto ON M1C 4B6 Canada**
**416-927-0355  www.innercitybooks.net**